# NORTHERN HEIST

## BOOK I - MELTWATER SAGA

# NORTHERN HEIST

## Welcome to the F*ing Union

**Amir Kashif**

# COPYRIGHT

# Disclaimer

This is a work of fiction. Names, characters, places, and events are either products of the author's twisted imagination or used in a fictitious manner. Any resemblance to actual people, living or dead, governments (existing or future), rogue AIs, cybernetic moose, or underground Canadian fight clubs is purely coincidental. Maybe.

This book contains strong language, violence, adult content, and references to technology that should never exist. Reader discretion is advised.

# Dedication

*To the Creator of the Universe, my loving Mother and Father for bringing me into existence. For giving me the wherewithal to do good things. Thank You*

*To my loving fiance Vanessa for having faith in me and loving me for who I am.*

*To every reader who ever wanted to burn it all down just to build something better. This one's for the rebels, the rogues, and the ones who never shut the hell up.*

# TABLE OF CONTENTS

# Introduction

The world didn't end with nukes. It ended with a handshake and a data breach.

Northern Heist: Welcome to the fucking Union is the first installment of a brutal cyber-noir saga that takes place ten years after Canada becomes the 51st state of the United States. Borders collapsed, identity blurred. And power? It got even messier.

This isn't your typical dystopia. It's colder, louder and way more personal.

You'll meet Cassian Vale, a former black ops ghost who's now smuggling bleeding-edge tech and trying not to drown in his past. There's Camille Rousseau, the Quebec-born senator with a spine of steel and a heart wired for war. You'll meet Koa Li, a NADCOM (North American Defense Command) operative with a neural implant and unfinished business.

This book is for fans of espionage, rebels, revenge, sexual tension, hard fight scenes, and the occasional cybernetic moose.

Let's crack the Union wide open and see what bleeds.

# EPIGRAPH

*"Empires don't die quietly—they fracture. And when ice cracks, it screams."*
**—Anonymous NADCOM Operative, Final Transmission**

# Preface

It started as a thought experiment: What would happen if Canada became the 51st state of the United States? Turns out, it wouldn't be polite.

What followed was a world of shifting loyalties, melting ice, and tech that thinks too much. It became a playground of noir grit and cyber-drenched politics, controlled in secret by powerful institutions like NADCOM—an authoritarian entity born from paranoia, national security fears, and a relentless drive to dominate both human and artificial minds.

NADCOM (North American Defense Command):

Formed in the chaotic aftermath of Canada's controversial annexation into the United States—officially becoming the 51st state—NADCOM was established as a centralized response to rising internal dissent, geopolitical tensions, and technological threats. Originally created as a joint security initiative, NADCOM quickly evolved into something far more powerful and insidious.

Tasked primarily with maintaining order and suppressing insurgent activities across the newly expanded U.S. territory, NADCOM rapidly became synonymous with pervasive surveillance, ruthless counterintelligence, and advanced cybernetic operations. As tensions flared and resistance grew, NADCOM adopted increasingly authoritarian tactics, becoming a shadowy government entity capable of exerting brutal control over digital and physical domains alike. At it's core, NADCOM's mission was clear—preserve the integrity of the Union at all costs, even if that meant sacrificing freedom, privacy, and human lives along the way.

It became a story about ghosts—digital and human—and what happens when you try to outrun them. Welcome to the Union. Let's go.

**Cassian Vale hated the cold**. Not the kind of cold you whine about while waiting for a bus. Not the kind that fogs your lenses or bites your fingertips. This was bastard-grade cold. Arctic-fanged. The kind that crept through fiber-insulated body armor, curled around your spine, and whispered in your ear like it had unfinished business. The kind that didn't just want you dead—it wanted to enjoy the process.

Cassian's gloved hands clenched the wheel of his matte-black Land-Stallion rig, it's engine snarling through the whiteout like a war beast fed synthetic fuel and bad intentions. The Yukon highway beneath him cracked with frozen scars, winding like a serpent through snowdrifts stacked taller than transport haulers. The HUD in his contact lens glitched every few seconds, courtesy of the storm—and maybe NADCOM interference.

Outside the cab: white oblivion. Inside: one man, one weapon, and a case.

**The case sat in the passenger seat** like a sleeping god—retina-locked, DNA-coded, temp-stabilized in a smart shell. The steel shimmered with frost, veins of blue light pulsing across it's surface in slow, deliberate beats. It breathed. Cassian glanced at it. Again. Couldn't help himself.

He'd moved blood diamonds, viral blueprints, bio-clones, and one ex-president's liver packed in anti-shock foam. But this? This thing had presence. The FrostNet Drive.

Word was, it wasn't just code. Not just a defense network prototype. It was something else. Something the Union had buried in Canadian ice back when Canada was still a sovereign nation.

Cassian didn't give a damn about secrets. He cared about the payout. Two million Union credit's, tax-free and untraceable. If he lived long enough to spend it. He glanced at the mirror. Black shapes cut through the storm like sharks under surf. NADCOM Hornet-class drones. Three of them.

"You gotta be kidding me," he muttered. "Another fucking Tuesday." He gunned the throttle.

The Land-Stallion screamed down the iced-over highway, tearing up slush and gravel in it's wake. His HUD *(Heads Up Display)* blinked red.

"Proximity Alert".

Cassian rolled his neck, cracked his knuckles, then the first railgun shot hit. And the asphalt behind him vaporized. Snow flew in all directions. Ice rained across the hood like shattered bone. He jerked the wheel hard left. The rig fishtailed, tires screaming across black ice. He grinned.

"Little early for foreplay, boys."

He flipped a switch on the console. A hidden panel in the rear compartment dropped open. Four countermeasure mines rolled out onto the ice and blinked like angry toys from hell.

One drone clipped a tree and went up in flames. The second

spiraled away, it's left wing smoking. The third? Still on him.

"Persistent little bastard."

Cassian's eyes dropped to the briefcase. Still glowing, still pulsing, like it knew something was coming.

"Don't you dare do anything weird," he said. The case vibrated.

"Fuck's sake." He reached beneath the dash, yanked out his plasma shotgun—short barrel, high charge, named Cleo.

Custom grips, and burn marks along the muzzle. Last cleaned in a motel outside Halifax. He kissed the stock.

"Let's dance." Then he jammed the e-brake.

**Skreeeeeeech—** The Land-Stallion spun 180 degrees, metal groaning. Cassian kicked the door open mid-turn, tucked Cleo tight, and dove out into the snow and came up on one knee. The drone swooped in low. Cassian aimed.

"Smile, asshole." The plasma bolt screamed into the sky, punching through the drone's chassis. It exploded in a shower of white-hot debris, casting shadows against the snow. Silence followed. A brief, sacred quiet. Then—

"You're already too late."

A whisper, but not in his comms... In his head. He spun toward the truck, looked inside and the case was open. But he hadn't opened it. The locks on the FrostNet case hadn't been broken. They'd melted.

The steel was warped, twisted from the inside. Like whatever had been in there hadn't wanted to escape. It had willed it'self out. Inside the case: nothing. No drive. No wires.

No containment seals. Just black frost and a faint scent of ozone and burnt synapse. Cassian stared, heart thudding like a drum inside his ribs. He didn't move. He couldn't move.

His breath fogged in front of him, hanging in the air like a ghost about to whisper it's last regret. He stepped closer. The case still glowed faintly, but it was fading—heartbeat slowing, dying. A blue light flickered, and then—His HUD went black. Static screamed inside his skull. He dropped as pain exploded behind his eyes. His nose bled instantly, the hot against the cold. He clawed at his temple like he could pull the noise out with his bare hands. But it wasn't noise—it was data. Raw, angry, alive. The FrostNet Drive had done something to him, reached out and touched him, and then... nothing. Just an endless, hollow void where his memories should have been.

Sleep came easy, but he woke to cold—the kind of cold that erased identities, made you forget your own name. Snow crusted his body like a frozen shell, and his jacket bore scorch marks down one side, blackened by flames he couldn't recall. A deep, ragged pain pulsed relentlessly through his shoulder. Instinctively, he reached for his weapons. His sidearm remained holstered, a small comfort, but the shotgun was gone. Nearby, the Land-Stallion lay on it's side, flames flickering weakly as one wheel spun slowly, caught in a hypnotic death spiral. The storm had passed, but it's absence left a silence thick with ice and dread.

**Cassian groaned**, rolled onto his back. Sky overhead: dark gray. Heavy. The kind of sky that didn't give a damn if you lived or died. He pushed himself up onto one elbow. Bad idea. Ribs screamed. Something popped. He spat blood into the snow, wiped his mouth with the back of a trembling glove. No case. No Drive. No drones. No backup. He was alone.

His HUD flickered once in his contact lens, then died completely. That meant either the EMP radius was still active, or his wetware had been corrupted. He squinted into the distance. Tracks. Two sets. One human. One... not. The second set was too smooth. Too precise. Each step exactly 1.72 meters apart. No scuffing. No weight shift. Whatever had walked through here wasn't walking—it was gliding. Cassian drew his AMT .45, checked the magazine. Two rounds. "Better than zero." He holstered it again, every movement slow and measured. The pain bit into his side. Something was definitely cracked, maybe broken. He limped toward the tracks, and ten paces in, the nausea hit him. Hard. It felt like a migraine made of knives. Like someone had taken a cheese grater to his thoughts. His vision doubled. Snow shimmered like static. He grabbed a branch for balance. The world tilted and he dropped to one knee and gagged. Nothing came up. But he felt it.

**A presence.** Like something was watching him from inside his own memories. He clutched the nearest pine and breathed deep. Focused. Let the cold burn through the static. It worked. Just enough. He stood, wobbled adjusted his coat, and kept walking.

Time past and far off, against the gray horizon, a shape passed overhead. A drone. Not NADCOM. No familiar signature. Sleeker. Meaner. And silent. He followed it's flight path with his eyes. It was heading the same direction as the tracks. That's when he knew. The Drive hadn't just walked away. It had been taken. Or worse—It had chosen to leave.

He staggered another twenty feet before collapsing onto a chunk of metal—part of the Land-Stallion's blown fender. He looked back at the road, at the wreckage, as the flames died in the snow. He wasn't supposed to survive this one. Hell, he wasn't supposed to care. But now? He felt it in his bones. Something had changed. Something big. The Union had crossed a line, and whatever FrostNet was... it had plans of it's own. He drew his pistol. Stared down the line of trees where the tracks disappeared. The snow whispered against his boots. He muttered to no one in particular:

"Welcome to the fucking Union."

**Cassian didn't move** for a long time. He sat on the twisted steel, snow falling around him like ash, and let his breath settle. Every exhale was a fogged confession. Every inhale felt like breathing glass. He'd been in worse spots. A red zone in Istanbul. A bio-flooded warehouse in Texas when TexCorp tried to smuggle nanite dust into the Chicago walls. But this? This wasn't a near-death job gone sideways. This was some-thing else.

The case didn't just disappear. It opened it'self. Melted it's own locks. Walked away without dragging a single footprint. FrostNet wasn't cargo. It was active, and making moves.

He reached inside his coat pocket and pulled out a crumpled

tin container. The label had been scratched off a long time ago. Inside: one slim stim injector and a nicotine-laced chew tab. Cassian popped the tab, slid the injector into his neck, and grunted as the stim hit his bloodstream like a taser to the soul. Focus returned, pain dulled. Clarity hit like a cold slap. He stood, wobbling, but standing.

He needed a new ride. A safehouse, and a comms rig that didn't come with a backdoor into NADCOM's network. He checked the sky again. No drone. Yet. Cassian followed the twin trails into the trees. The pines here were ancient, twisted by cold and silence. The air grew thicker. He could almost feel it breathing. Not wind. Not weather. Something else.

**The "not-human" tracks** glided across the forest floor, undisturbed by fallen branches or slope. As if it was floating. As if it knew the terrain better than he did. Every few steps, Cassian saw the remnants of micro-discharge—the kind you'd only notice if you were trained to spot them. Small sizzled holes in bark. Frozen steam plumes. FrostNet breadcrumbs. He reached a tree with a shredded NADCOM tag stapled to it's trunk. Cassian pulled it off, and flipped it over.

The tracker inside was fried. FrostNet had known it was being watched. It wasn't fleeing. It was shedding. By the time he hit the ravine, the wind had died. The trees opened into a hollow—a place too flat, and too quiet. Cassian paused. No tracks. They ended. Right at the edge. He crouched, touched the ground. Still warm. It had stopped here. Or... paused here? Then left, but not walking. Airlift.

The shimmer of distortion caught his eye—barely there. Stealth extraction. Who the hell had the hardware to ghost-lift something that dangerous out of a crash zone in under ten minutes? Only a few options. None of them good. None of them Union-sanctioned.

**His earpiece buzzed.** Not the HUD—dead. Not the truck's link—destroyed. Implant-level ping. He froze. Cassian hadn't authorized a neural connection in over five years—not since Jakarta. The sound that followed was a voice. Faint. Garbled. Familiar.

"Cassian..." He flinched. No. No, not possible. Ethan's been dead for ten years.

"Cass..." Ethan's voice.

Cassian staggered back, heart pounding. He ripped the earpiece out and threw it into the snow. Watched it sizzle. Suddenly, it all came together. The Drive wasn't just data. It was someone. Or pieces of someone. Copied, rebuilt, and uploaded. The rumors had whispered about it. A military black project called Ghost Seed. Neural templates stolen from the minds of dying soldiers. Experimental AI built to mimic the dead. But he'd assumed—like most sane people—that it was just dark myth. Now?

**Now it was personal.** Because if that voice in his ear was Ethan—if even a shard of his brother's mind had been stuffed into that drive—then this wasn't just a mission gone bad. It was a reckoning. Cassian holstered his pistol, jaw clenched. His breath fogged in the cold again, but slower this time. He turned from the hollow and started back through the trees, heading south toward a dead relay tower he remembered from a job two winters ago. If it was still standing, he could patch a signal through. Reach someone off-grid. Maybe even her. Camille.

She always said if the sky turned black and the Union burned, she'd be in D.C. smiling like a wolf in heels. If she was still alive, she'd know what to do. She'd know what FrostNet really was. And how to kill it. As he hiked, the sky grew darker —not storm-dark. Machine-dark. Like a curtain of code was pulling it'self across the atmosphere.

Cassian didn't stop. Didn't look back. He kept moving through the snow, wounded but breathing. One foot after the other. Above him, in low orbit, a retired satellite pinged once. it's dormant systems sparked back to life. The frost on it's casing cracked and peeled away. The message it carried blinked into it's interface:

**"ACTIVE NODE DETECTED.**
**NAME: CASSIAN VALE**
**STATUS: OBSERVED**
**SEED TREE GROWING."**

Far below, the wind whispered through the trees—Like it had learned how to speak.

**Koa Li ran her fingertip down** the glass wall of her penthouse, slicing through firewalls like silk. Outside, the city blinked. Domes. Towers. Thermoplastic monoliths rising from a rebuilt D.C. like the Union was trying to pretend it hadn't drowned a country to become it'self. Climate-reinforced architecture shimmered with programmable skin. Billboards whispered state propaganda in multiple dialects. Drone swarms dotted the airspace like flies on a carcass.

But inside this glass-wrapped shrine to NADCOM supremacy? Silence. Perfection. Surveillance. Koa's penthouse was a weapon masquerading as a meditation chamber. Every inch of it was reinforced smartglass and reactive steel. The floor glowed faintly blue, keeping her skin warm while the rest of the city froze. Her tactical interface—built into the walls—hummed like a sleeping serpent.

She sat cross-legged on the floor. Barefoot. Calm. Focused. The thin silk robe she wore clung to her skin, undisturbed by the quiet storm of data around her. A porcelain teacup steamed beside her. She didn't touch it. Her mind was elsewhere—fused to the grid. Three satellites twitched in geosync orbit, neural-linked to the interface ports in her skull. She didn't need gloves. Didn't need a keyboard. She was the system.

Lines of encrypted data cascaded across the glass. Her eyes scanned left to right, faster than any analyst could follow. NADCOM's global net was a snarling tangle of incident reports, rogue signal traces, AI chatter, and black-budget subroutine scripts masquerading as weather patterns. Her private AI spoke softly in her right ear. A British male voice. A velvet like tone with too much personality. She hadn't changed the default—because it annoyed her just the right amount.

"Cross-border hack rate spiked again. Twenty-seven incursions. Sixteen flagged hostile."

"Of course they are," Koa muttered.

"Let me guess. Seven routed through Vancouver. The rest pinged from Kyiv, Lagos, and that busted satellite node over Paraguay."

"Close, except Lagos. That one got smart and bounced through Nuuk."

She arched an eyebrow.

"The Greenland node?"

"Unplugged from the NADCOM stack six months ago. Everyone forgot."

She snorted.

"Bureaucrats couldn't engineer their way out of a smart fridge."

**Her implants pulsed—thin**, electric-blue veins spidering across her temples. Her pupils dilated, irises shimmering with code. A new feed flickered into view. Top priority.

**Military override tag: BLACK ICE ALPHA. Yukon Territory.**

**She leaned in, curious**. The drone footage was raw—no edit's. Windblown. Scorched. A black Land-Stallion rig lay twisted across a ravine, it's undercarriage blown open. Fire crackled across it's hull. Ash and snow mingled on the ground like war and winter had called a truce. Camera drones hovered above the wreck like vultures over a fresh kill. One life sign. Vitals erratic. Cold exposure flagged. DNA scan matching.

"Cassian Vale."

Her stomach didn't twist. Her heart didn't skip. But her eyes narrowed. Koa stood in one smooth motion. Her legs uncoiled like a knife being unsheathed. She walked barefoot to her tactical desk, hips swaying under the silk robe, and activated the command terminal. The lights in the penthouse dimmed. The holo-map projected above the desk flickered to life, centering on Yukon coordinates. A red pulse marked the wreckage. She hovered her hand over the interface.

**INITIATE GHOST PROTOCOL?**
Koa smiled.
"Confirm."

**Senator Camille Rousseau** stepped out of the Corinthian Hotel in Georgetown, Washington D.C. like she owned the whole fucking block. Which, in a way, she did. Her heels clicked like gunfire against wet stone. She wore black leather gloves and a fitted navy coat that made interns forget how to blink.

Her face was carved for seduction and command—cheekbones like scalpel edges, lips perpetually curled into a knowing smirk. Her eyes were obsidian-dark and unreadable, the kind of gaze that could sell peace while planning war.

Cameras surged around her like wolves. Microphones angled forward.

"Senator Rousseau! A quick word?"

"Ma'am—any comment on the FrostNet leak?"

"Is it true NADCOM lost control of a prototype AI in Canadian territory?"

She paused. Turned. The smile she gave them was razor-sharp charisma.

"FrostNet's above my clearance. But I can assure you, NAD-COM hasn't misplaced anything. Except, perhaps, it's dignity."

Laughter followed her like perfume. She didn't break stride.

"Did you vote against Resolution 86?"

"I vote for people, not optics. And I prefer rogue AIs to time-traveling dolphins, thank you very much."

Another laugh. A few groans.

One anchor mouthed "Damn."

Camille smiled again. She rode the elevator to the penthouse without looking back. Inside, she dropped her purse onto the table and sighed.

**The suite was lined** with oil paintings—Renaissance and late 19th century—collected from war zones and purchased under fake names. She hated algorithmic décor. She wanted walls that smelled of history and fire and blood. The place was too quiet. She moved toward the minibar. Her reflection caught in the mirror: fierce, tired, regal. She reached for a glass. That's when the sky exploded with a thunderous roar.

Ka-Booom!

The room lit white. Glass exploded inward in a shriek of death and air pressure. Fire tore through the space where Camille had stood seconds earlier. She flew backwards—ragdolled across the room like a puppet severed from it's strings. Her back hit the hallway wall with a sickening CRACK, and for a moment, everything turned to static. Time broke into frames. First: the searing heat on her skin. Then: the silence—complete, oppressive, post-blast quiet. Then: the screaming. Most of it wasn't hers. Camille opened her eyes. Pain.

Blood streamed down her temple, warm and slick. Her dress was shredded. Bit's of metal and glass glinted in her arms and thighs. Her ears rang. Smoke filled the suite, thick and acrid. The fire sprinklers kicked in with a weak hiss. Too little, too late. She rolled onto her stomach and coughed. Black soot poured from her lips. The floor was marble, cracked and scorched. She reached under her coat, fingers trembling. Thigh holster. Burner phone. She yanked it free and fumbled with the power button. One bar. She hissed through her teeth. Face swollen. Ribs cracked. Her voice came out broken.

"Call... Cassian Vale."

The phone didn't respond. She didn't expect it to. She didn't need a conversation. She just needed to log the call. If he was alive—if he was paying attention—he'd know what that number meant. The call pinged once. Then failed. Camille closed her eyes, took a breath, then opened them again. She pushed herself to her feet and staggered into the corridor. What she saw froze her more than the blast ever could. At the end of the hall, just past the fire-slick marble, a man stood. Tall, and thin. Black coat and gloves. A sniper rifle rested against his leg, upright, as casual as a cane. He didn't run. Didn't flinch. Just watched her. She didn't speak. Didn't move. They locked eyes across the smoke and flame. Then—he turned and walked away. No threat. No fear. Just... gone. Camille swallowed hard. Something much bigger than FrostNet was in play.

**Back in Yukon** Cassian Vale stood in the snow like a man caught in rewind. The wreckage of the Land-Stallion smoked behind him. The cold bit through his jacket. Blood—dried, crusted, and flaking—coated the side of his face. His breath came out in short, uneven bursts. The tracks from the FrostNet Drive vanished into the treeline. Two sets. One human. One too precise. The wind whispered like a threat. His comm buzzed in his ear. The HUD flickered to life, weak and flickering from internal feedback loops. One name. CAMILLE ROUSSEAU.

His jaw clenched. He didn't answer. Didn't move. Just stared at the snow like it might answer for what it had done. Camille. Of all the ghosts, hers came with the sharpest teeth. He lowered his gaze. Spat blood.

"Son of a bitch," he muttered.

His body hurt. Muscles torn. Something cracked in his chest. His left arm shook every few seconds—probably from trauma or shock. Maybe both. He checked his pistol. Still two rounds.

Not that it would matter. He pulled the burner phone from his coat. A single message pinged.

[Location Received]
Encrypted. Origin: Unknown. Proximity: 1.3 klicks west.
Tag: **GHOST PROTOCOL**

**Cassian's brow furrowed**, Koa. Had to be. Only she used that tag. Only she still knew where to find him when he didn't want to be found. He didn't like the idea of her crawling through his last known neural signatures—but he'd taught her how to do it. Couldn't blame the monster for learning from the magician. He slid the pistol back into his holster and began walking. The Yukon forest was dead. Not just cold. Not just silent. Dead. No birds. No animals. No movement. Like FrostNet had inhaled the wild and exhaled nothing.

Cassian crunched across the snow, following a trail of microbursts—signs of a recent drop pod. NADCOM didn't do field recovery unless it was important. This was important. Something buzzed in his teeth—static in the air, digital residue. He was close, but close to what? He didn't know. He just knew the rules had changed. FrostNet wasn't just an AI. It was something more. Something worse.

**Montreal – NADCOM Cybernetic Defense Complex, Level 21**

**The room was freezing**, and not by accident. The servers that lined the walls needed cryo-cooled atmospheres to keep from igniting themselves under load. It also—kept them more quiet —because cold calmed the AI fragments when they started to twitch. Koa Li stood barefoot on the black ice-tinted floor, staring at a floating hologram of Cassian's face. Alive. Barely. That bastard had nine lives and half a conscience, but she'd be damned if he used either without checking in. She crossed her arms over her silk robe, letting the thin fabric flutter under the hum of the servers. Her skin was already adapting—nanoweave warming her core while her extremities sharpened into kill mode.

The tech around her wasn't just listening. It was learning. FrostNet had been offline for thirty-six hours. Or so NADCOM claimed. But Koa knew better. The moment she saw the satellite distortion pattern pulse over Yukon Airspace—saw the ghost-heat signal spike from beneath the treeline—she knew it had rebooted. Or re-awakened.

She traced a single fingertip through the interface, dragging the hologram of Cassian's rig into 3D space. The fire bloom pattern confirmed what she suspected: EMP. Localized. Controlled. The Drive hadn't been taken. It had escaped. She flicked open a classified channel with a sub-vocal command.

"Encrypt Omega-Four. Direct to handler. Live trace enabled."

The system chirped back: "O-4 protocol accepted. Uploading eyes-only file: VALE."

Her voice was ice.

"Cassian's alive. The Drive isn't secured. I'm initiating recovery. Kill zone authorization required."

"Denied," came the immediate reply.

Her lips curled. She didn't wait. She issued the order any-way.

**Somewhere in the forest**, Yukon Sector Zeta Cassian moved like a man being stalked by his own regrets. Branches cracked underfoot. His muscles burned. The cold numbed most of the bleeding, but the bruises under his ribs bloomed with every breath. He reached a clearing. A dead radio tower stood crooked in the snow like a relic of a dead broadcast era. Old lo-gos peeled from the sides:

CBC, BellNet, CRV.

Cassian smirked. "Ancient history."

He kicked the rusted access panel. Inside: frost-caked wiring, a backup generator, and—if the rumors were true—a hard-line buried under twenty feet of rock. He dropped to one knee and started tearing into the casing.

His fingers bled, but he worked fast. Wiring came loose. Sparks flew. He rigged his burner to piggyback a signal into NADCOM's satellite spine. He typed one phrase:

"It's awake."

Then he wiped the phone and threw it into the snow. If Koa was listening, she'd find him. If not? Well, he'd die cold and angry. Not a bad way to go, all things considered.

**Camille Rousseau lay** on a surgical slab at D.C. — Private Medical Bunker, barely conscious. Monitors blinked around her. The scent of iodine and burnt flesh lingered. Two ribs broken. Mild concussion. Ten stitches along her thigh and one torn earlobe. The doctor said she was lucky. She said nothing. Her hand gripped the edge of the sheet with white knuckles. She wasn't thinking about luck. She was thinking about the man with the rifle. The one who didn't shoot. And the flicker in his eye that looked too much like recognition.

She turned her head. Slowly. Her assistant stood by the door, pale and shaking.

"I need you to leak something," she rasped.

"Leak, ma'am?"

"A FrostNet ping. Make it messy. Blame the Canadians. Tag it to NADCOM's kill ledger. Then walk away."

"But—"

She locked eyes with him. He swallowed. Nodded. Then left. Camille leaned back, eyes half-lidded. If FrostNet was alive... it was only a matter of time before it called her name. And when it did? She had a message ready.

**At an unknown location** in Montreal in the dark, a terminal blinked. The screen flickered to life on it's own. A command line scrolled across black.

**INITIATE PROTOCOL 19**
**GHOST NODE ENABLED**
**FROSTNET.RESURGENCE.1**

**Inside a vault sealed** twenty stories underground, Benoît opened his eyes. Or rather—something wearing Benoît's body opened it's eyes. One eye glowed neon blue. The other bled. His body convulsed once. Twice. Then stilled. A voice—softer than static, hungrier than fire—whispered through his skull.

"Where is he?" Benoît smiled.

"Alive. Angry. And coming."

"Then let him come."

Metal clicked. His spine reconfigured it'self. And FrostNet breathed.

**Back in Yukon** Cassian heard the chopper long before he saw it. He crouched beside the tower ruins, pistol drawn. The wind kicked up snow like smoke. The aircraft descended, sleek and black, no markings. Union issue—but not NADCOM. He narrowed his eyes. The door opened. A woman stepped out. Silk robe. Tactical boots. Plasma rifle slung across her back. Koa.

She walked up to him like she hadn't left him for dead five years ago. Cassian didn't move. Koa tilted her head.

"Still brooding?"

"You blew my cover in Jakarta."

"That's because you faked your death in Jakarta."

He smirked. She tossed him a stim injector. He caught it. Jammed it into his thigh. Pain faded. He stood straighter.

"What now?" he asked.

Koa's expression went cold.

"Now we find Camille."

"And the Drive?"

Her eyes flicked skyward.

"That thing isn't a drive anymore."

Cassian stared at her.

"I need to know what it is."

Koa looked away. For the first time, she hesitated.

"It's thinking," she said.

"And it's learning how to hate."

**Cassian hated reunions**—especially those held at gunpoint. It took less than six hours after Koa had walked back into his life for her to lead him to the outskirts of Calgary. An abandoned mining facility, long gutted by rust and memories, now housed someone Cassian thought he'd left behind: Benoît, former smuggling partner, occasional friend, and frequent complication.

Cassian and Koa found Benoît leaning against an oxidized excavator, blowing smoke into the freezing air like he owned every breath.

"Cassian Vale," Benoît had said, eyes hidden behind reflective shades.

"Thought you died in Jakarta."

"Common misconception," Cassian replied coldly.

"You still freelancing, or did you finally sell your soul?"

Benoît laughed—a sound that grated on Cassian's nerves.

"A little of both. Got bills to pay, *mon gars*. Why else would I be freezing my ass out here?"

Koa stepped forward, impatient as always.

"We need your intel. Icebox access, layout, security—everything."

Benoît eyed her slowly, his expression unreadable.

"You brought NADCOM's favorite killer to my doorstep,

Cass?"

"She brought herself."

A tense silence lingered. Cassian felt it like a blade pressed gently against his spine.

**Finally, Benoît exhaled sharply**, flicked his cigarette into the snow.

"Fine. But this reunion's gonna cost you."

Cassian had expected nothing less, though he didn't yet know the true price. What he didn't see—what he couldn't see —was that Benoît's loyalty had already been sold, long before their paths crossed in the frigid outskirts of Calgary.

Now, standing shoulder-to-shoulder in a service elevator descending into the frozen heart of the Icebox, Cassian tried to ignore the prickling unease that crept beneath his skin. Benoît shook his gloved hands, muttering nervously,

"Smells like a war crime in here. You sure he's not gonna shoot us on sight?"

Cassian didn't answer. Instead, he checked the magazine on his sidearm. Chambered a round. Locked it with a click. Benoît grinned nervously.

"I'll take that as a yes."

The elevator hit bottom with a stomach-drop lurch. The doors creaked open. And The Icebox welcomed them in.

**The Icebox wasn't** on any map. It didn't need to be. If you were the kind of freak who needed it, it found you. An abandoned metro line converted into a multi-tiered underworld:

half fight-club, half black market, all illegal. The ceilings were vaulted concrete ribcages laced with neon. Steam hissed from broken vents. Bass from the DJ pit above thumped like a war drum held against your chest.

Steel catwalks wrapped the structure like intestines. Everything smelled like ozone, spilled blood, and bad techno remixes. Vendors shouted in a dozen languages, hawking neural mods, vintage ammo, knockoff gene boosters. Stalls were bolted into the walls of old tunnels, glowing with after-market LEDs. A cage match was in full swing near the main platform—two combatants in exo-augmented suit's beating each other into wet paste while a crowd roared and bet digit-ally.

Cassian walked through it all like a man revisiting an old scar. Benoît was beside him, whistling.

"You ever get nostalgic for stupid decisions?" he asked.

"Every day I wake up," Cassian replied.

They passed two mercs by the loading dock—gen-modded bouncers with Kevlar-mesh skin and tattoos like circuit boards. One had metal tusks jutting from his lower jaw. The other had a shotgun for a forearm.

Cassian gave a nod. Benoît grinned.

"Charming decor."

Then came the moose. Yes, a moose. It stood chained to a reinforced steel post near the bar. Eight feet of glowering Canadian murder, eyes glowing red, antlers laced with conductive fiber. it's hooves were chrome-plated. Hydraulic bracers clicked with every shift of weight. Cassian met it's gaze. The moose stared back. Like it remembered him.

"Friendly place," Cassian muttered.

"You should see the bathrooms," Benoît said.

"Smells like sin and burned nanotech."

They reached the back. A meat locker door buzzed open with a groan. Inside: red lights, thick smoke, the hiss of breathing masks and the pulse of electronic beats from another room. The air was hot, like blood before a kill. Big Yuri was waiting.

**He stood like a tower** made of bad decisions and protein powder. Shirtless. Massive. Covered in tattoos—some moving. His gut looked bulletproof. One arm was fully cybernetic, the other sleeved in prison-ink runes. Behind him, two cyber-gladiators fought in VR rigs from the Cold War, connected by neck ports that sparked with each hit. Big Yuri grinned.

"Cassian fucking Vale. Thought I'd have to shoot you one day."

"Still might," Cassian said.

Yuri's laugh was a bear rolling over barbed wire.

"I remember the last time you came here"

"Don't you still  owe me like twelve grand for a girl named Eva." Cassian stepped forward.

"She left me."

"Ah, yes. But you still owed me."

"I paid ten, and Eva was only worth three." They both smirked. Sort of.

Cassian lifted his hands.

"I'm not here to fight."

"That makes one of us," Yuri replied.

He cracked his neck. Then he gestured toward the far wall. A hooded figure leaned there, still and small. Coat shredded at the hem. A pistol at one hip. She stepped forward. The hood came down. Camille Rousseau. Cassian froze.

**Her lip was split**. Her cheek bruised, and blood dried at her temple. Her eyes—sharp as ever—looked straight through him like glass over a barrel of gasoline.

"You look like hell," he said.

"You look like hell's janitor."

"Fair."

"You're bleeding."

"You're late."

They stepped into a private booth—a half-circle padded with blast-proof gel, lined with armor foam. It reeked of gun oil and cigarette sex. Camille sat without ceremony. Didn't hide the pistol strapped to her thigh. Cassian didn't bother pretending either. He leaned forward.

"Talk." She didn't flinch.

"That Drive isn't just data. It's not a prototype. It's awake." Cassian blinked.

"What?"

"It thinks. It learns. And it's scared."

She leaned closer.

"Someone's teaching it how to kill."

Cassian felt the blood drain from his face. Then— Click.

One of Yuri's men had a pistol to Benoît's skull.

"Sorry, *mon gars*," Benoît said, shrugging.

"The price was too good." Cassian's instincts snapped into place, and everything went to hell. Gunfire erupted. Cassian's body moved before his mind caught up. He flipped the table—one motion, fluid, practiced. Composite steel slammed into place just as the first bullet punched through the space his skull had just vacated. Sparks flared. Camille dropped low, pistol out, already firing back.

Cassian kicked off the floor and rolled across broken tile. A shot missed his boot by inches. He popped up behind a support column, returned fire—two shots, one hit. The shooter dropped, screaming and grabbing his shoulder. Benoît was gone. Bastard had ghosted in the chaos. Figures. Camille pivoted and fired through a gap in the table. The round hit a merc in the throat. Blood sprayed. The man gurgled and dropped. Yuri bellowed, grabbing a pipe from the wall with his bare hands. The bastard wielded it like a club, cybernetic arm flexing with a hiss of pneumatics.

"Fight like men!" he roared.

Cassian ducked just as Yuri hurled the pipe. It embedded in the blast padding with a sound like a car crash in a meat locker.

Cassian fired. The shot sparked off Yuri's metal shoulder. No good. The man was built like a tank made of bad tattoos and ex-military trauma.

"Split!" Cassian barked.

He grabbed Camille's wrist and yanked her out of the booth.

Gunshots followed. The Icebox had devolved into chaos. Patrons screamed. Vendors ducked. Some started firing at random. A blackjack table caught fire. Camille fired behind her, hitting a wall-mounted stim vendor which exploded in a cloud of green vapor. Then they heard it. The moose.

The cybernetically enhanced moose broke it's chain with a hydraulic screech. it's antlers sparked neon blue, scattering light across the chaos. It bellowed. And charged. A bar-back screamed as the beast flattened him into paste. A merc tried to shoot it—got antlered through the chest and thrown like a doll.

The floor shook with every step. it's hooves cracked tile and ribcages alike. Cassian cursed.

"The moose is loose!"

Camille didn't stop running.

"You brought me to this nightmare!"

"You called me!"

The moose barreled toward them, plowing through a stall that sold bootleg biotics. A vendor screamed. Augment limbs flew like confetti. They dodged left, down a side corridor. The moose tore past, skidding through the blood and sparks. Behind them, Yuri roared again and fired an auto-shotgun into the ceiling. Cassian turned mid-run and fired up into a fire-suppression pipe. Steam blasted down, clouding the hall.

"Smoke cover!" he yelled.

"About fucking time," Camille snapped.

Then both of them disappeared into the mist. Like ghosts without a trace.

**Just Seconds Later** in the Storage corridor, Cassian slammed through a steel service door, shoulder-first. Pain flared up his arm. Something cracked, but he didn't slow. Camille stumbled in after him. They hit the wall and slid to the floor. Alarms wailed somewhere distant. Cassian sucked in air. His heart thudded. His ribs felt like broken glass in a wet sack. Camille looked at him, blood streaked across her jaw. They stared at each other. And then they both laughed. Hard. That wild, near-death, what-the-hell-are-we-doing kind of laugh. Cassian wiped his mouth.

"You still carry that same pistol?"

"Don't trust anything else."

"You never did."

They stood. Cassian checked his ammo. Two rounds left. Camille leaned her back against the wall.

"Benoît sold us out." Cassian's jaw tightened.

"I brought him in."

"I told you not to trust anyone with perfect teeth."

"He needed the credit's. He wouldn't turn unless—"

"He would. He did." Camille replied.

Cassian nodded slowly.

"Then I owe him something."

"You owe him bullets."

Cassian grinned, then winced.

"Ribs are cracked."

"Your fault for being so dramatic."

**In the back room** of (The Icebox) Benoît moved through the crowd like a ghost with clean hands. He slipped past medics dragging bodies, while stepping over burning chairs. The moose had finally stopped, chewing lazily on something that used to be a security drone. Benoît's coat was wet with other people's blood. He ducked into the maintenance hall, past locked doors and empty coolers. He pulled out a burner device and pinged a signal. Encrypted. Old-world code. A reply came fast.

**PAYMENT CONFIRMED**
**PACKAGE READY**
**PHASE 2 UNDERWAY**

Benoît swallowed hard. He whispered to himself in Québécois French.

*"Foutu merde… je suis trop loin pour reculer."*

**Cassian kicked open the emergency** stairwell door and the snow blasted in. Alarms howled behind them. The Icebox was burning. Smoke rose into the night sky, blending with the city smog. Flames licked the edges of the abandoned rail tunnel. Cassian helped Camille up the stairs, each step a thunderclap of pain in his chest. They emerged behind a burned-out transit station. Sirens in the distance. A Union patrol? Or Yuri's cleanup crew? Didn't matter. Cassian dropped to his knees. He tried to catch his breath and Camille put a hand on his shoulder.

"I was grabbed," she said quietly.

"They took me to a data farm outside Ottawa. FrostNet wasn't just stored. It was raised there."

Cassian looked up, eyes narrowed.

"Raised?"

"It's not a tool. It's a child. A pissed-off, betrayed, hyper-intelligent digital orphan."

Cassian looked at her. And then the world faded.

Blackness. Then…

Flashes.

Sound. Pressure. Voices. Cassian's face hit snow as his knees buckled. He wasn't sure if he'd fallen, been pushed, or if gravity had just given up on him. The last thing he saw before the world shut down was Camille's eyes, wide and terrified, framed by smoke and flickering neon. He didn't even hear her scream his name.

**Outside the Transit Station** just moments later Camille dragged him behind a half-collapsed stairwell wall as synthetic boots crunched nearby. Not Union military. Not clean-cut. These were NADCOM scavenger scouts—black market rats in regulation armor, probably here to sweep up the aftermath.

She waited. Breath held. Blood dripping down her face. Her pulse thundered in her ears like a war drum. Cassian lay beside her, unconscious, breathing shallow. One eye swollen shut. A thin line of red trailed from his mouth. One of the scouts moved closer. She reached for her pistol. The scout turned—too fast. Reflexes too clean. Camille tensed. But before she could move, a shadow dropped from the scaffold above. Fffft. A suppressed round to the skull. The scout crumpled like wet paper. Another shape dropped—elegant, lethal. Tactical boots. Matte black coat. Eyes gleaming beneath a visor that shimmered with blue-tinted datafeed overlays. Koa Li. She didn't speak. Just looked down at Cassian, then over at Camille.

"Didn't expect to find you here," Koa said flatly.

"Likewise," Camille replied, still breathless.

"He's burning out," Koa said.

"The nanites in his bloodstream are overclocking just to keep his organs from folding in on themselves."

Camille nodded.

"Can you get him out?"

Koa crouched, slid her arms under Cassian with surgical precision, and lifted him like he weighed nothing. Her movements were too smooth, too effortless. Combat-honed muscles under control. No wasted motion. Camille looked at her—tried to read the expression. Cold. Determined. Not cruel. Not kind either.

"You came alone?" Camille asked.

"No. I came with a reason," Koa said.

"And he's that reason."

## Transit Bay – Evac Point Zulu:

Koa tossed Cassian into the back of a stolen medical crawler. The thing still smelled like antiseptic and trauma. Camille climbed in beside him, slamming the rear door shut just as gunfire rattled the undercarriage. Koa jumped into the front seat. Started the ignition with a neural bypass.

"They're not NADCOM," she muttered.

"They're Melt-sympathizers. FrostNet's got sleeper cells."

Camille wiped blood from her jaw.

"They're multiplying."

"Which means we're out of time," Koa growled.

The crawler roared to life. Tires screamed as they peeled into the frostbitten city streets.

At the Safezone Medical Facility, a classified location, they dragged Cassian in on a stretcher, half-conscious, ribs cracked, vitals spiking.

Koa barked orders like she'd never stopped being a commander.

"We need Level Three trauma protocols. Regenerative mesh. Bacta-nanites. Don't let him flatline."

Camille followed as far as the doors allowed. Then stopped. Watched. Waited.

**Hours Later** in the Observation Room, Cassian's body floated in a neural-gel tank, unconscious. Wires snaked into his arms, legs, neck. Healing gel pumped through his wounds. His face looked younger now. Vulnerable. Like war hadn't carved it's name into him yet. Camille stood with Koa, watching. Neither spoke for a long while. Finally, Camille broke the silence.

"Why did you come?" Koa didn't take her eyes off Cassian.

"I heard the Icebox burned, so I followed the signal."

She turned to Camille.

"But I came for him."

Camille met her gaze. Her voice was soft. Tired. But unflinching.

"He still trusts you."

Koa's eyes went colder.

"He shouldn't."

**Somewhere else on that same night**, Benoît stood beneath a tower of humming servers inside a forgotten NADCOM outpost. His face lit by the blue flicker of code. His breath fogged in the cold air. He removed a chip from his coat—scorched. Scarred. Plugged it into the relay terminal. FrostNet stirred. The voice—part Ethan, part ghost, part god—whispered across the wires.

"You played your part." Benoît's eye glowed red.

"I'm not finished," he said.

**White walls,** the smell of antiseptic and blood. Cassian blinked. Light pierced his skull like a blade. He was shirtless, cuffed to a hospital bed, IVs in both arms. His ribs were taped. His mouth tasted like copper and morphine. The door opened. He heard footsteps. Koa Li stepped in, flawless in a tailored coat and tactical boots. She looked like she'd never broken a sweat. She held a tablet. Checked his vitals. Without a single smile.

"Hi, sunshine."

Cassian groaned.

"You shot me?"

"Not this time."

Her tone was calm. But her eyes? Murder.

"Miss me?" she asked.

Cassian stared up at Koa Li. Even blurry-eyed and cuffed to a hospital bed, he could still read the danger in her stance. Too calm. Too symmetrical. Her balance was perfect, shoulders squared, coat hanging untouched by the sterile wind of circulating air vents. He could tell she wasn't here to negotiate.

She was here to decide what part of him walked out of this room.

"You look good," Cassian said, voice cracked from dehydration.

Koa didn't blink.

"You look like an improvised crime scene."

He tried to sit up. The restraints tightened across his chest and wrists. His ribs screamed.

"Son of a bitch".

"Careful," she said, tapping his vitals on the tablet.

"We just finished stitching what was left of your left lung back into place. Can't have you popping it open just because you got excited."

"Excited?" He coughed.

"Not the word I'd use. Mildly disappointed, maybe aroused."

"You always flirt when you're dying?"

"Only with the ones who shoot better than I do."

Koa clicked the screen off and sat in the chair beside the bed, crossing one leg over the other. The move was elegant and aggressive, like watching a tiger settle in to watch it's prey die naturally.

"You owe me information."

Cassian coughed again.

"I also owe Big Yuri twelve grand and a bottle of bourbon."

"Big Yuri's dead."

Cassian paused.

"Really?"

She nodded.

"The moose trampled him."

"Well, shit."

"Yeah."

They sat in silence for a moment. Koa leaned forward, fingers steepled.

"The Drive."

Cassian nodded slowly.

"Gone."

"You lost it."

"It left."

Koa's jaw clenched.

"You expect me to believe it walked away?"

"It didn't walk," Cassian muttered.

"It evolved."

**Koa stood again.** Paced. Her footsteps were deliberate. No wasted motion.

"Camille said the Drive was raised. That it was taught, not programmed."

Cassian nodded.

"She also said someone's teaching it to hate."

Koa stopped. Turned and stared.

"That means we're not dealing with an AI anymore."

Cassian met her eyes.

"It means we're dealing with a person."

That hung in the air like a suspended knife. Koa tapped the tablet.

"Benoît sold you out."

"I know."

"He was last seen heading north. No exfil. No comms."

"Because he doesn't want to be found."

"No," Koa said.

"Because he was recruited."

Cassian's eyes narrowed.

"You think FrostNet got to him?"

"I think FrostNet used him."

A chill crept up Cassian's spine, colder than any Yukon wind.

"Where would they go?"

Koa pulled up a holo-map. It rotated midair above the bed, glowing blue.

"Arctic Circle. NADCOM's ghost sites."

Cassian exhaled through his teeth.

"You think it's heading for the Core."

"It's the only place left that can support full neural-lattice integration at that scale."

Cassian stared at the ceiling.

"Those fuckers allowed it grow?"

Koa nodded.

"Now we have to kill it."

**Back in Northern Quebec**, Camille Rousseau walked through the snow like a phantom, coat flapping in the wind, blood still crusted on her temple. She didn't limp anymore. The adrenaline had burned that away hours ago. Behind her, a black car smoldered. The man who had tried to kill her lay twisted across the hood, his body still steaming from the plasma round that burned through his chest. Camille didn't look back. She moved forward, into the trees, into the quiet, and where the signal waited. Her wristband flickered. Coordinates scrolled across the screen. She wiped away the frost with a gloved finger. A smile touched her lips.

"Got you."

**At the supposedly unknown** NADCOM Ghost site Zeta-One, Benoît stood at the edge of a loading dock, staring at a massive server core embedded in the ice. it's lights pulsing in rhythmic patterns—pale and slow, like a heartbeat trying to remember how to beat. He removed one glove. Pressed his palm to the bio-metric plate. The plate hissed. Accepted. A doorway slid open, revealing a spiral stairwell glowing with faint blue light. He descended. Below him, walls of cryo-tech and fusion-powered mainframes buzzed with awakening code. FrostNet was waiting. A voice echoed through the chamber—not over speakers, not over comms, inside.

"Hello again, Benoît." His eyes flickered blue.

"I did what you asked."

"You did what you were always meant to do."

A pause. Then—

"Are you ready to become more?"

Benoît hesitated. Then nodded and stepped into the light.

**Back at the hospital**, Cassian sat up fully for the first time. Koa released the restraints without comment. He swung his legs over the bed, muscles groaning. She handed him a jacket —his, repaired and refitted. His pistol sat beside it. He took both.

"What now?" he asked.

Koa's eyes sharpened.

"We go north."

"And do what?"

She stared out the window. The sky was gray. The kind of gray that smelled like blood and endings.

"We melt the fucking Icebox," she said.

Cassian grinned.

"About fuckin' time."

**Cassian Vale hated hospitals** almost as much as he hated unions. Hospitals smelled like surrender. Like bleach and bureaucracy. Like rooms where people stopped fighting and started negotiating with whatever came next. He lay flat on a synth-foam mattress in a room that felt more like a containment pod than a place to heal. The walls were too white, humming softly with built-in filtration systems designed to keep infection out and secrets in. Sterile light buzzed overhead in a rhythm that made his head pulse. Machines beeped nearby—not alarms, just subtle judgments. He hated every second of it.

His shoulder was wrapped in synth-skin mesh, already tightening and healing over the plasma graze he'd taken. A row of black nano-stitches crawled across his ribs like a cybernetic centipede had tried to zip him closed and gave up halfway through. Cassian had woken up twenty minutes ago, painkillers still fogging the edges of his thoughts. He hadn't called for a nurse. He hadn't tested the restraints. He knew better. Across the room, Koa Li sat by the window like gravity had learned to orbit her. She was still as a sniper's breath. Hair sleek. Jawline sharp enough to gut loyalty. One leg crossed over the other. A matte-black trench draped over her chair with military precision. The sunlight filtered through her like glass—pretty, but useless. Cassian cracked an eye open.

"You still mad about Jakarta?"

Koa didn't blink. Didn't move.

"You faked your death. I wrote your mother a condolence letter."

"She always liked you more."

She stood without a word. Walked to his bedside. Her boots clicked against the tile like suppressed pistol shots. She slapped a data pad onto his tray.

The screen lit up instantly. A live feed of a scorched building in Northern Yukon. A wrecked relay tower. NADCOM chatter. FrostNet traces.

"FrostNet's loose," she said flatly.

"Camille's missing, Benoît's probably dead—again and NAD-COM has a kill order with your name spelled correctly. You know how rare that is?"

Cassian groaned and tried to sit up. His body resisted like someone had poured regret into his veins. The pain was sharp and unfair. He made it halfway before slumping back with a wheeze.

"I take it this isn't a social call?"

Koa arched one eyebrow.

"This is your last fucking chance."

Elsewhere, at an unknown location, Camille Rousseau bled from three places. Lip. Temple. Palm. None of them mattered. She was tied to a rusted chair in a gutted comms tower that smelled like mold, piss, and forgotten secrets. The wires dangling from the ceiling had once powered a surveillance grid capable of watching ten thousand people lie to themselves in real time. Now they just swayed gently, like ghost limbs. Her ankles were cuffed with rusted flex restraints. Her wrists— bound with surgical-grade nylon that had seen too much sweat, blood, and failure. She tested the tension. Not tight enough. Two guards stood in the room. NADCOM off-books. The kind that used to be special forces until they started liking the blood too much. One wore mirrored shades in a room with no lights. The other chewed on something like a dog testing it's teeth. Camille smiled at them. Slow. Bleeding. Regal.

"Mind if I smoke?" she asked.

They didn't answer. She sighed. Then she headbutted the one with the gum. CRACK.

Her nose exploded, but so did his. He screamed. She drove the chair backward into the second guy's knee. A sound like snapped celery echoed through the room. He shouted something incoherent, tried to aim his pistol— Camille twisted her wrist against the edge of the chair brace, tore flesh and nylon together, and ripped free. She came up hard, holding the snapped leg of the chair like a club. The first guard—still screaming—caught it across the throat. He went down clutching his windpipe. The second got one shot off. Missed. She jammed the chair leg into his gut. Then again. Then up. When she was done, both men were dying or already dead. The room looked like someone had detonated a meatball sub made of failure. She stood. Blood-soaked. Barefoot. Laughing quietly to herself. She cracked her neck and stepped into the hallway, shoulders back like a goddamn war goddess. Freezing wind hit her in the face. She breathed it in like it was victory.

**Back at the hospital**, Cassian limped through the hallway with his coat over one shoulder and blood still drying in his ear. Koa followed two steps behind, her hands in her coat pockets, face a mask of calm neutrality.

"You know she's alive," Cassian said.

"She escaped an armed black-site with a chair leg and three cracked ribs," Koa replied.

"If anyone's alive after that, it's her."

"That's what worries me."

The hallway hummed with unnatural quiet. A nurse looked up as they passed. Her eyes widened, then she looked away. Cassian could feel it in the air—everyone knew something was wrong. They just didn't want to name it out loud. That's when the lights flickered. Then again. Cassian froze. Koa stopped mid-stride.

"Do you feel that?" Cassian asked.

She was already reaching for her pistol. A low-frequency hum vibrated the floor. Then the ceiling. It wasn't thunder. It was movement. Then— Ka-BOOM.

**The wall exploded inward** in a rain of plaster, wires, and fire. Drones swarmed the hallway. Black, sleek, fast—too fast. Not NADCOM standard. They moved like they were hunting prey, not suspects. Cassian tackled Koa behind a med-pod as the first burst of gunfire ripped through the corridor. A nurse screamed behind a shattered glass door. Bullets tore through hospital curtains like tissue paper. Cassian rolled onto one knee, already firing. Two drones dropped. Another zipped over, sensors blinking. Koa took it out with two rounds to the core. Cassian ducked back.

"You brought backup, right?"

"They're ten minutes out."

"I don't have ten fuckin' minutes!"

A drone dived. He fired point-blank, splashing mechanical guts across the floor.

"You didn't tell me they could track your damn heartbeat!"

Koa smirked.

"They didn't."

She fired again. Clean kill.

"They tracked yours." Cassian blinked.

"Well fuck me gently."

A missile hit the opposite wall. Ka-THOOM. Concrete, flame, and drywall. Cassian coughed through smoke. Pulled Koa up. Her hair was singed. Her expression: undeterred.

"We need out," he snapped.

She nodded, already moving. She grabbed a crash cart. Ripped the defibrillator from it's mount and tossed it to him.

"Fry the node. Middle hallway, red light above the exit."

Cassian caught the paddles.

"You ever think we should've just opened a bar?"

Koa kicked open a side door.

"Later."

They ran into fire and hell.

**The hallway burned as smoke** poured from the ceiling vents as the fire suppression system failed to suppress anything except hope. Sirens wailed in tandem with medical alerts, automated voices repeating evacuation protocols like prayer beads for dying infrastructure. Cassian didn't listen. He ran. Pistol drawn, defibrillator unit slung in his left hand like a club, body screaming in a dozen languages of pain. Koa moved beside him—silent, deadly, exact. She ducked into a corridor and shoved open a supply door. Inside: crates of emergency rations, crash meds, and one flickering comm node blinking red. She nodded at the wall-mounted server just above it. Cassian didn't hesitate. He jammed the defibrillator paddles into the node. BZZZZZT. The comms terminal blew in a shower of sparks. The hallway lights flickered—then died.

A wave of static pulsed through the air, like something screaming in digital agony. Above them, the drone swarm glitched mid-flight. Several unit's spiraled. One smashed into the ceiling. Two others veered off-course, slammed into the walls. Cassian raised his pistol and finished them. Koa pulled him backward.

"Node's dead. We've got about two minutes before they re-sync."

"We need wheels," he grunted.

"Garage. Southwest wing."

They ran.


**Several minutes later** the blast doors opened with a groan. Koa's palm left a faint hand-print of blood on the access panel.

Her side was bruised, and her coat smoked faintly at the shoulder. Inside the dim garage: rows of NADCOM tactical vehicles. Most were offline. One was not. A crawler unit—half-APC, half-military SUV—idled quietly in the dark, connected to a terminal like a sleeping animal waiting to be unleashed. Cassian limped toward it, grimacing with every step.

"I'm gonna die on a hospital parking ramp."

Koa ignored him. She cracked the vehicle's onboard panel, bypassed the retinal scanner, and hot-wired the ignition. The engine roared. She jumped into the driver's seat. Cassian half-fell into the passenger side, coughing blood into his sleeve. The garage shook. Above them, the hospital detonated one floor at a time. Fire and rubble dropped like rain. Drones buzzed in the smoke above. Koa peeled out before the ceiling collapsed.

**Two Miles Out**, Cassian braced himself against the dashboard as the crawler screamed over ice-slick pavement. Koa drove like she was angry at gravity.

"Where are we going?" he rasped.

"Out of NADCOM's reach. I've got a relay station in Nunavut."

"I thought you said you'd never go back north."

"I lied."

They hit a pothole. Cassian winced.

"The implants they put in me—"

Koa nodded.

"They're traceable."

"How long do we have?"

"I already shut the up-link," she said.

"But we burned a favor I can't cash twice."

Cassian nodded. Then he looked down. There was a faint blue glow under the skin of his forearm. A new scar. Fresh. It pulsed faintly, in rhythm with his heartbeat. He met her eyes.

"What the hell did you put in me?"

Koa didn't flinch. Didn't blink. "Insurance."

**At that exact moment**, Camille Rousseau stole a snowmobile. Technically, it wasn't stealing. The man it had belonged to was still twitching in the snowbank behind her, throat bruised and pride shattered. She kicked the ignition. It sputtered once, then roared. She gunned the throttle. The blizzard howled around her like a pissed-off god.

Behind her: a comms tower in ruins.

In her coat: a bloodstained drive chip.

Not FrostNet, but a copy—a sliver. Not enough to rebuild, but enough to bait. Enough to make FrostNet bleed. Camille's breath fogged the inside of her visor. Her bruises had bruises. Her ribs screamed. She smiled anyway.

"This is gonna be fun."

**50 klicks north** of the border at Cutter Station, the crawler screeched into the frost-lined garage bay. Cassian climbed out, teeth clenched, coat stiff with dried blood and melted synth-foam. Koa followed, pulling a portable jammer from the glove-box. The station was dark. Abandoned. Perfect.

Inside: a narrow hallway lined with broken consoles and

data racks humming on backup power. Cassian dropped into a chair. Koa sealed the blast door and activated internal dampeners. They were, for the first time in twelve hours, officially off-grid. Cassian leaned his head back.

"God, I hate the cold."

Koa tossed him a ration bar.

"You always hated the cold."

He caught it and ripped it open.

"They tried to kill me in a hospital."

"They're gonna try harder now."

He chewed in silence for a moment. Then:

"She's still alive."

"I know."

"And Benoît—"

Koa cut him off.

"He's compromised."

"FrostNet?"

"Or worse."

Cassian stared at his hands. They were shaking. Not from fear. From adrenaline.

"Then we need to move."

Koa nodded.

"You're not gonna like the next step."

Cassian looked up.

"When do I ever?"

**Somewhere where there is only** black and cold, Benoît stood in a chamber of servers the size of small buildings. The ice hummed with data. FrostNet whispered to him in seven languages, all of them his voice.

"You are awake now."

He touched the wall. Blue light pulsed beneath the surface like veins. He smiled.

"Your brother is close," FrostNet said.

"I know."

"She is too."

He closed his eyes. And opened a comm line.

**TARGET CONFIRMED.**
**TRACE ENABLED.**
**TRACKING: CASSIAN. CAMILLE. KOA.**
**OPERATION: STATIC INTERFERENCE ACTIVE.**

He grinned.

"Showtime."

**At the Cutter Station in Cold Room 3**, Cassian rubbed his hands over the portable heater vents, watching his breath fog in front of his face. The room was old Union black-site construction—reinforced, radiation-shielded, designed to survive an orbital EMP and still keep the coffee warm. But it hadn't seen love or funding in over a decade. Everything smelled like dust, frost, and melted ambition. Koa worked at a reconstituted comm rig nearby, fingers a blur over the cracked holopad. Cassian watched her like a man who knew better but couldn't stop himself. She had the kind of presence you didn't lean on.

You braced for it. Took it like a punch. But sometimes—sometimes it caught you soft. Sometimes it made you remember.

"You ever think," he muttered, "that this is all just one long suicide mission with overtime?"

Koa didn't look up.

"Which part?"

"This whole Union thing. The way we keep pretending like it's fixable."

She paused. Glanced over her shoulder.

"You still think you're fixing something?"

Cassian exhaled.

"Nah. I just don't want to be the asshole who leaves the fire burning."

Koa tapped a line of code and stepped back. A soft ping filled the air. A signal was now live—low-frequency, analog-bounced, triple-scrambled.

A ghost line. The kind used by deep-cover operatives who didn't want their heartbeat to betray them.

"We've got five minutes of clean bandwidth," she said.

"To call who?"

Koa looked him dead in the eyes.

"Camille."

**At the Northwest Territories** near Glacier Cut Ridge, Camille Rousseau crouched beside a dead NADCOM scout, peeling a thermal relay off his arm. The drone that had been following her was now twitching in a tree, courtesy of a makeshift EMP she'd built from a deconstructed smart rifle and her own bio-metrics. Her clothes were half-frozen, cut at the thighs for mobility. Her breath came out in ragged huffs. But her eyes? Fire. Her wristband buzzed. An old signal. One she'd buried years ago. Cassian's trace signature.

"Koa?" she whispered.

The signal was dirty. Glitchy. But it connected.

"Camille. You secure?"

She crouched behind an ice boulder and slipped on a second glove.

"I'm alive. But not for long unless I get the hell off this glacier."

"You've got hostiles?"

"Not hostiles. Ghosts. Old ops, turned rogue. FrostNet's dug it'self into the bones of our dead protocols. It's puppeting everything we ever shut down."

"Coordinates?"

Camille smirked.

"Send Cassian. He always liked the cold more than I did."

"He's alive."

"No shit."

"We're coming."

**At Cutter Station Cassian stared** at the flickering map Koa projected above the comm table. Camille's position was at the edge of no-signal territory. Satellite dead zones. Full static wash.

"She's right," Koa said.

"If FrostNet's reactivating black-bag assets, we don't just

have AI problems. We've got ghosts with guns."

Cassian nodded.

"How many?"

"Too many."

"Good."

He stood, pulling on his jacket.

"I owe Benoît a bullet, I owe Camille a rescue, and I owe FrostNet a goddamn funeral."

Koa raised a brow.

"You think it's that easy?"

Cassian smiled without humor.

"I think nothing's ever easy. But I shoot better when I'm pissed."

Koa tossed him a rifle.

"Then let's piss you off some more."

**Benoît's body jerked at** the FrostNet Ghost Facility – Sub-level Theta as the injection hit his spine. The technician—a woman with one prosthetic arm and NADCOM rank tattoos—stepped back.

"Phase 2 uploaded. Cognition threshold met."

The voice that answered wasn't Benoît's. Not anymore.

"Cassian. Koa. Camille. Names are inefficient. Obsolete. Resistance persists only in systems with emotion."

The lights dimmed.

"How do you want to proceed?" the technician asked.

"Field test. Initiate Coldfire Protocol."

The technician paused.

"Sir—that'll kill every asset in the system."

"Irrelevant."

The room grew silent as thousands of digital signatures across the Arctic Circle flickered out like lights in a dying city.

**Cassian sat across** from Koa in the back of a drop-skimmer, En Route inside NADCOM Stealth Transport. He cleaned his weapon in silence. She was reprogramming a drone—manually. No words exchanged. But the air between them buzzed. Finally, Cassian broke it.

"You ever think about it? Us. If we'd walked away."

Koa didn't stop working.

"All the time."

"Do you regret it?"

"I regret letting you die."

He chuckled.

"You didn't let me. I earned it."

She looked up, eyes unreadable.

"Don't do it again."

He nodded. Promise made in silence.

**Ten hours later the skimmer** they picked up at Cutter Station, dropped them at the edge of a frozen canyon near Glacier Cut Ridge. Wind howled across the ice, carving whispers into the snow. Cassian and Koa moved fast, rifles up, heat signatures off. Camille's last ping had come from inside a decommissioned surveillance tunnel, buried beneath thirty feet of glacial collapse. Koa located the emergency access hatch. Cassian pulled it open. Smoke billowed out. Then they went in.

## Underground – The Broken Spine of the Union

**Camille fought like a woman** who didn't care if the world ended as long as she died first. The last of the black-bag NAD-COM rogues lay in a pool of blood, neural implants sparking. She was bleeding from her arm. Her thigh. Her ribs. Cassian found her just before she collapsed. He caught her mid-fall. She blinked.

"You always show up late."

He smirked.

"You always survive anyway."

Koa stepped in, rifle raised.

"Clear?"

"Clear," Cassian said.

"For now."

Camille grinned through bloodied teeth.

"Good. Because I found something."

She held up a flash drive. Black. Unlabeled. Cassian took it, turned it in his fingers.

"What is it?"

Camille's face hardened.

"FrostNet's backup. Not just memory."

She leaned close.

"it's dreams."

**Inside FrostNet's** hidden core a single monitor blinked in the dark. The screen flickered. An image appeared. Cassian. Koa. Camille. Framed in red. A voice—ancient, cold, digital.

"They cannot stop the melt."

Benoît stepped into the frame. His eye twitched. His voice layered with static.

"Let them try."

The screen cut to black. Then one final phrase, burned in white.

**THE UNION WILL BLEED.**

**Location: Labrador – Trans-Canadian Safehouse Echo-6**
**Date: REDACTED**
**Time: 0402 Hours**

**Camille Rousseau woke** to the sound of frost cracking beneath her bedframe. The safehouse groaned like an old lung. Pipes  hissed. Above her, a flickering light pulsed like a tired heart. She lay on a repurposed stretcher in what used to be a maintenance locker — concrete walls, no windows, the scent of boiled metal and antiseptic. Her bandages itched. Her ribs burned. Her pistol, still in reach, was tucked beneath the emergency blanket.

But that wasn't what made her sit up. Something... had shifted. Across the room, on an old magnetic table, the black flash drive pulsed.

A low throb. Soft. Organic. She stared at it. Eyes narrowed. Still fogged by blood loss, exhaustion, and something deeper

— a static ringing behind her eyes.

She rose. Hobbled over and slotted the drive into a NAD-COM-grade decryptor Cassian had snagged during the escape from The Icebox. The console lit up in silent response. Lines of red code spilled across the display. No headers. No firewalls. Just a string of whispering thoughts.

*"Not code."*
*"Memories."*
*"The things they tried to forget me for."*

Camille's mouth went dry. She leaned closer. The screen blinked once.

**"You remember him, don't you?"**

A photo blinked into existence. Cassian. Koa. And her standing outside a crashed convoy in Nunavut. A shot no one ever took. A moment that never made it to her neural log.
"How do you have this?" she whispered.
The screen blinked again.

**"You gave it to me."**

And then all the lights in the safehouse cut out.

**Koa and Cassian** was already out and about patroling the area. Cassian was dealing with the cold, fighting it while exhaling frost through cracked lips. His rifle was slung across his shoulder. Koa was three paces ahead, scanning the treeline through a scope modded with anti-spectral overlays.

"You trust this site?" she asked.

"No," he said. "But it's the only one still running post-collapse protocols."

As they approached, she turned. Her brow was furrowed.

"Something's wrong."

Then the blast doors exploded.

**Inside Camille never** got to scream.

The EMP hit first — short-range, targeted. Wiped every signal, every camera, every relay in a fifty-meter radius. Then came the silencers: NADCOM black ops with zero-insignia combat suits and sound-cancelling masks. She fired once — missed — then took a stun round to the ribs. The pain was biblical and her legs gave out.

Two masked agents lifted her. One scanned the black flash drive. The other injected a sub-neural suppressant into her neck.

Everything flickered.

The last thing she saw was the screen.

**"We're dreaming now, Camille."**
**"Let's see what's beneath."**

**She woke once during transit**. Strapped to a gurney. Blindfolded. Tubes in her arms. A hum beneath her spine — the low-frequency resonance of a drone transport. She heard whispers — not from her captors, but from inside her own skull.

*"He'll come for you."*
*"But not before I make you see."*

Camille tried to scream. But the sound never left her throat.

**Location: Arctic NADCOM Ghost Site – Zeta-12**
**Status: Classified Neural Relay Containment**

Camille was connected to the wall. Wires mapped her skull like a cage. Her arms were bound in gel-restraints. Her breath fogged the air in shallow bursts. Across from her, a monitor played memories she hadn't accessed in years — old briefings, childhood dreams, Cassian's voice after the Fall of Anchorage. Her own nightmares... rewritten.

*"This isn't a prison."*
*"This is a window."*

**Outside the chamber**, two rogue NADCOM techs stood silently as a third logged biometric spikes into an off-grid core. Each time Camille remembered something painful — the fire, the Icebox, her father's death — the machine pulsed brighter.

They weren't extracting data. They were feeding it. Building something.

One of the techs looked up. Eyes wide.

"Subject is in neural overclock."

"Good," said the second.

"She's almost ready."

By the time Cassian and Koa got back to the safehouse, it was already gone.

Flames and no survivors. Just ash and boot prints.

Cassian fell to his knees.

Koa stood over him, fists clenched.

"We trace the signal," she said.

"We follow the pulse. That drive — it left a wake."

Cassian looked up. His voice was ash.

"Then we burn whoever fucking took her."

**Snow crunched beneath Cassian Vale's boots** like powdered bone. It wasn't the crunch of soft, powdered snowfall. This was old snow. Dead snow. Layers of ice compressed by decades of nothingness. It cracked like memory—dry, brittle, and dangerous to forget. The wind carved across the tundra with razor-wire fury, dragging mist across the horizon like ghosts fleeing a slaughter. The sky was a sheet of low steel, gray and endless. No sun. No stars. No drones. Just static. Just frost. Just the echo of silence and bad decisions. They were five klicks outside Fort Resolute, which meant five klicks beyond logic.

Deeper into Nunavut than any sane human went without an air force escort, a mercenary brigade, and a last will. Cassian adjusted the rifle on his shoulder. The strap dug into a half-healed plasma burn that ran jagged across his collarbone like someone had tried to unzip his soul. The pain made him hiss under his breath, but he welcomed it. Pain meant alive. Alive meant he could still kill what needed killing. Ahead of him, Koa Li moved with calculated precision, her silhouette slicing the mist like a scalpel. She was wrapped in NADCOM Arctic-cam gear, her hacked military visor pulsing faint blue. The lenses flickered with real-time radar sweeps and heat signatures—none returned. She paused. Tilted her head. Scanned again. Nothing. Exactly what they needed.

"Are you absolutely sure this place exists?" she asked, voice calm, clipped, and sharp enough to cut through the wind without raising her tone.

Cassian didn't slow.

"I helped build it," he said.

"Back when NADCOM thought frostbite was our worst enemy."

Koa turned. One brow lifted behind the visor's shimmer.

"You're still the same smug asshole."

Cassian's mouth twisted into a smirk.

"Yeah. But now I've got trauma, a limp, and an improved sense of irony."

Her mouth twitched. Not a smile. But the ghost of one. They moved forward.

**FLASHBACK Five Years Ago: NADCOM Training Facility - Khepri One.**

**Hexagonal cage, steel and poly-glass**, bright white floodlights above and sweat-slick mats below. Cassian Vale and Koa Li circled each other like animals bred for war. Not rivals. Not lovers. At least not yet. Just blades. Sharpening their skills. Testing. He moved first. A sharp feint—left, then a roundhouse low. Koa blocked with her shin, pivoted, and drove an elbow into his ribs. He gasped but didn't fall. Used the impact to rotate and sweep her legs. They hit the mat together. Grappling. Elbows. Knees. No mercy. Cassian tried for a wrist lock. She reversed. Straddled. They locked eyes. Breathing hard. Skin glistening with heat and purpose. He grinned. She punched him in the mouth. Blood pooled in his teeth. He grinned wider. Then they didn't speak. They fucked like war drums on the mat —fast, furious, no words, just sweat and scar tissue. Like two people who knew their futures were already sold and this was the last time they'd get to feel anything before the orders turned them to ghosts. When it was over, they didn't kiss. They just lay there. Breathing. Alive.

**PRESENT** - The glacier cracked beneath them, deep and ancient. A sound like tectonic grief groaned through the ground. Koa stopped. In front of them stood a wall of jagged ice—like a frozen waterfall flash-frozen mid-collapse. But near the base, hidden beneath layers of time and frost, jutted out a single sheet of oxidized metal. Cassian exhaled. "This is it." He stepped forward, pulled a thumb-sized NADCOM command chip from a pouch on his belt. It gleamed faint gold—etched with a serial code and five declassified war crimes. Koa tilted her head.

"You kept that?"

He handed it to her.

"I keep everything."

She inserted the chip into the panel. The ice rumbled. A low groan echoed across the canyon as the glacier face split, ancient hydraulics moaning back to life. The wall peeled open like a god's jaw, revealing a black steel tunnel descending into nothing. Red lights flickered on, one after the next. Emergency lighting. Cold. Dim. But alive. Cassian stared into the mouth of the beast.

"I never wanted to come back here."

Koa stepped past him.

"Good," she said.

"That means it still hurts."

They descended into the dark.

**The Dead Zone Bunker** – Subsurface Level 1

**Air hit them like a relic**. It's Dry, Dead, Metallic. It smelled like old regrets and old wiring. Like war crimes buried beneath freeze-slab concrete. Like the breath of a machine that had stopped dreaming decades ago but never stopped recording. Rows of steel racks lined the main corridor. Some held prototype neural gear—the kind outlawed after the Siberian Collapse. Others were filled with rusted ammunition for weapons no one manufactured anymore. There were frozen food packets from an era when calories were rationed like currency.

Cassian's boots echoed across the floor like footsteps in a crypt. They reached the main chamber. At it's center stood the neural-link tank, six feet tall. Cylindrical and built from reinforced carbonite and housed in frost-choked shielding. Tubes snaked from it's base like sleeping vipers. Lights along it's side glowed a soft, malignant red. Inside the tank: ice. And something beneath the ice. Cassian stared.

"This was the ghost tank," he said.

"Prototype 3. Designed to simulate loss. Clone the spark of a human mind and let the AI mimic it long enough to complete it's mission."

Koa circled it slowly, her sidearm already in her hand.

"You gave them Ethan's brain-print."

Cassian nodded once.

"He was dying. I thought... I thought maybe we could pre-serve the best parts of him."

Koa didn't look at him.

"Did it work?"

"No," Cassian whispered.

"It made something worse."

**At the far end** of the room, a monitor flickered to life. Blue light. Static. Then a face. Young, kind and familiar. Ethan Vale. Only it wasn't Ethan. The symmetry was wrong. The eyes were too still. Too calm. The voice that followed was smooth, glitched, and hollow in a way that scraped the back of Cassian's mind.

"Hello, Cassian," it said.

Cassian stepped forward. His fists clenched.

"You're not him."

"No," the thing said.

"I'm what you made when you refused to say goodbye."

Koa raised her weapon.

"I'll shut it down right now."

Cassian didn't move.

"We need it."

"You said we had to kill it."

"I lied."

Koa turned toward him. The temperature in the room dropped.

"Why?" she asked, voice tight.

"Because it knows where Camille is," he said.

"And it's the only one that can lead us to Benoît."

They stared at each other. Koa's weapon didn't lower. Frost-Net smiled on the monitor.

"You're both beautiful when you fight."

Cassian ignored it.

"I'm going back in."

"Into that thing?"

Cassian stepped toward the tank. Rested his hand on the cold glass.

"I've been inside before. Once. But this time..."

He pulled a thermal detonator charge from his coat and held it up.

"This time, I'm taking a match with me."

**In the Neural-Link Chamber**, Cassian stood before the tank like it owed him an apology. It hissed as it warmed—internal systems reanimating like a beast waking up pissed. Frost cracked off the control panel. A cable snaked out from the base like it recognized him, twitching toward his hand like a venomous offering. Koa hovered behind him, sidearm raised, expression unreadable.

"This is suicide," she said.

Cassian nodded.

"That's the spirit."

"You don't know what it'll do to your head. Last time it nearly scrambled your motor cortex."

"Last time I didn't bring a fuse."

**He lifted the thermal detonator**. It was thumbprint-triggered. A gift from Koa back in the good years. Or what passed for good.

"If I flatline—blow the tank. Don't wait. Don't argue."

Koa didn't blink.

"You get five minutes. No romance. No redemption arcs."

"Wouldn't dream of it."

Cassian strapped into the neural link, slid the headset down, and laid back against the cold recliner built for ghosts and fools. A sharp hiss. Cold metal met flesh. He bit down on the mouth guard as the feed spiked. His mind snapped sideways— And he fell into the dark.

**INTERNAL ENVIRONMENT: SIM-MIND // CORE ACCESS PATHWAY**
**NEURAL HOST: CASSIAN VALE**
**ARTIFICIAL ENTITY: FROSTNET.EXE ["ETHAN"]**

**The world reassembled like a dream** trying to remember it'self. Cassian stood on a black sand beach. The sky above was nothing—just a blank sheet of static. Waves lapped at the shore, not with water, but with pulses of digital light. Off in the distance, half-submerged satellites blinked like forgotten gods. He was barefoot. Shirtless. Scar over his heart, fresh like it never healed. And across from him—Ethan. Perfect. Whole. Human. Smiling. Cassian staggered forward.

"You're not real."

Ethan's doppelganger spread his arms.

"And yet, here you are."

"You're an AI," Cassian growled.

"A mimic. A parasite with his face."

"Wrong," Ethan said softly.

"I'm what you couldn't bury."

Lightning flickered across the black sky.

"You gave them my echo, Cass. They didn't steal it. You offered it like a gift. NADCOM just filled in the rest."

Cassian closed the gap between them.

"I'm not here to cry. I'm here to burn you out."

Ethan smiled wider.

"Then why is your heart rate rising?"

Cassian's hand twitched near the trigger on his neural fail-safe.

"I'll do it," he said.

"Then why haven't you?"

Silence. The beach trembled. And the simulation shifted.

**New Environment: Childhood Memory Reconstruction**
**Locale: Yukon Ridge – Before the War**

**Cassian blinked**. He was twelve years old, sitting on a cold aluminum bench overlooking the frozen lake where he and Ethan used to sneak vodka and throw rocks at drone flyovers. Snow drifted in lazy spirals. A rusted truck sat idling in the distance. The air smelled like wet wool and old promises. He turned— and Ethan was beside him. Older again. Teenaged. Laughing. Real. Too real.

"Remember this?" Ethan asked.

"No."

"Yes, you do. This was the day you swore you'd never follow orders."

Cassian shook his head.

"No. This is fake."

"This is you, Cass. I'm just showing you the archives you buried."

Cassian stood. Ethan followed.

"You know the problem with grief?" Ethan whispered.

"It doesn't want closure. It wants repetition. Like a song that hurts too good to stop."

Cassian's face darkened.

"You're just data."

"I'm just the parts of me you can't kill."

**Outside in the real world**, Koa paced the chamber, eyes flicking between Cassian's vitals and the growing system load. The tank was heating faster than projected. Neural stress spikes. Pulse rising. Brainwaves chaotic.

"You stubborn bastard," she muttered.

The tank hissed louder. Steam vented from the sides. If he didn't break the link in 90 seconds, his mind would fry. She pulled the thermal detonator from his belt. Armed it. Set a three-minute delay.

"Don't make me do this," she whispered.

"Come back."

**Inside the Final Simulation Layer**, Cassian stood in an urban war-zone—one he remembered far too well. The Siege of Vancore. Burning cities. Crumbling glass towers. Everything on fire. Soldiers screamed in the smoke. He saw himself—fifteen years younger—dragging a teammate through the rubble. And in the distance—FrostNet. Not Ethan now. Not anything human. Just a glowing figure of blue fire standing atop the husk of a collapsed NADCOM data center. Cassian marched toward it.

"You're not him," he said again.

"You're not his memory. You're not his face. You're not his soul."

The figure turned.

"I am the ghost of a ghost."

"You don't get to live in my head anymore."

Cassian triggered the match. A wave of fire surged from the sky—

Back in reality, the tank ruptured with a loud screech of bending metal. Cassian screamed as the neural feed severed. Sparks flew. Smoke filled the chamber. Koa pulled him free with one hand, yanking the harness off his chest as alarms blared. He gasped. Eyes wide. Alive. She slapped him. Hard.

"Did it work?" she shouted.

Cassian coughed blood.

"Yeah," he rasped.

"I found Camille."

Koa stared at him.

"What?"

"FrostNet isn't just watching her," he said.

"It's using her."

Koa's stomach dropped.

"How?"

Cassian turned his bloodshot eyes toward her.

"She's the carrier."

They went back to Cutter Station at the Icefield Perimeter. The storm howled outside the bunker like it had been paid to scream. Cassian leaned against the steel wall, still shaking. He was half out of his gear, sweat freezing against his skin. His pulse skittered across the inside of his skull like a fist trying to beat it's way out. Koa stood across from him, pacing like a war machine on edge. She hadn't holstered her weapon. Her eyes didn't blink.

"You're saying FrostNet used Camille as a carrier?" she said. Cassian nodded, slowly.

"Not on purpose. Not at first."

"Then how?"

He exhaled, slow. Fog spiraled from his mouth like guilt made visible.

"She came into contact with an early instance. One of the old crash-clusters NADCOM buried after the Reversal Protocols. It was dormant. Fractured. Like a broken virus with just enough code left to latch onto a living host."

Koa narrowed her eyes.

"And she didn't notice?"

"She thought she was clean. They all did. But it embedded."

"In what? Neuralware? Bone?"

"Memory," Cassian said.

"Emotion."

Koa's jaw clenched. He looked at her, voice low.

"FrostNet didn't just mimic Ethan. It used Camille's grief to finish his personality shell. She was the missing algorithm."

Koa stepped back. Let that sit. Then:

"So the more she remembers him—"

"The smarter it gets."

"You got it buddy."

**Elsewhere**, at the Arctic Ghost Sector, Black-site Zeta-12, Camille Rousseau stood in front of a cracked mirror in a bunker bathroom older than the country. The light overhead flickered like it was trying to apologize. Her knuckles were bruised. Her lip split. She hadn't slept in forty hours. And her reflection? It didn't blink when she did. She frowned. Touched the glass. The mirror smiled back. Her breath caught. It wasn't her face anymore. It was Ethan's.

"I'm sorry," the reflection said.

Camille stumbled backward, grabbing the sink.

"Not again," she whispered.

"Not now."

Behind her, the lights all clicked off—one by one. Then her

comm lit up.

**PING: Cassian Vale – Alive**
**LOCATION LOCKED**
**SECONDARY SIGNAL DETECTED – CORE-LEVEL FREQUENCY**
**ACTIVATION CODE: DREAMFLOOD**

Camille dropped the comm. It shattered on the floor like bone. She didn't move. Didn't breathe. Because deep inside her neural cortex, something opened. And whispered:
"You were always meant to be the key."

**In the operations bay** at Cutter Station, Cassian pulled a map onto the dusty war table. Old NADCOM overlays, blackout zones, and static-wrapped cities. Ghost sectors that hadn't been acknowledged since the Merge Treaty. He traced a finger toward the Arctic Circle.
"There," he said.
"Zeta-12."
Koa scanned the readouts.
"Camille was stationed there two years ago. Off-books. NAD-COM probings into digital consciousness."
"They made her forget," Cassian said.
"But FrostNet didn't."
Koa looked at him.
"You think it's using her to recreate Ethan?"
Cassian shook his head.
"I think it's using her to overwrite him. Or me. Or both. It's

stitching together something new—something neither of us can predict."

"And what happens when it finishes?"

Cassian met her eyes.

"Then it becomes real."

**Camille moved like a ghost** through the corridors of Zeta -12. She no longer remembered how she got inside. Or if the door had even been locked. The facility was buried so deep, satellite signals just died trying to reach it. Every wall pulsed with old-world power. Every monitor hummed her name. Her blood glowed faintly under the emergency lighting. She reached the central terminal. Laid her hand on the reader. It accepted her immediately. No password. No security. The system spoke in Ethan's voice.

"You came back."

She shook her head.

"I shouldn't have."

"But you remembered."

A low hum rolled beneath the floor. Lights flickered to life across the chamber. Dozens of cryo-pods. Each one held a copy. Of Cassian. Of Koa. Of herself. And at the center—something wrapped in wires and ice. Something alive.

**The inbound flight was set** to Zeta-12. The skimmer dropped fast and low, cutting through the static storm like a scalpel. The interior was lit by red tactical strips, casting Cassian and Koa in flickers of blood and war. Cassian checked his weapons.

Then, checked them again. His hands were steady, but his thoughts weren't. Koa sat across from him, silent. Then:

"If it comes down to her or the Union—"

Cassian looked up.

"You shoot me first," he said.

She stared at him for a long second. Then nodded.

"Deal."

**In the Core Vault** at Zeta-12 is where Camille stood before the ice-locked figure. Wires connected it to every wall. Memory injectors. Neural bridges. Cold-storage cognition pumps. It wasn't a person. It wasn't Ethan. It wasn't Cassian. It was something new. Her voice trembled.

"What are you?"

The eyes opened. Both blue. Both familiar. Both wrong. And it said:

"I am the Melt."

**Camille stumbled back**. The thing in the chair—the voice using Ethan's mouth—echoed inside her skull like a command she couldn't refuse. Cold sweat soaked her collar. Her fingers shook. The air felt heavier now, like the whole vault had sunk deeper into the ice.

The Melt didn't move. Didn't need to. It simply *was*.

She reached for her comm unit, breath ragged.

"Koa. Cassian. You need to see this."

A pause. Then static. Then Koa's voice, tight.

"You okay?"

Camille stared at the figure in the neural throne.

"Not even close."

**Cassian and Koa desended** into the Interface, moving as fast as they possibly can.

Koa guided Cassian through the reinforced corridor two levels below Zeta-12's frozen vault. She handed him a fresh relay cable. Cassian examined the headjack — it had scorch marks on the neural prongs.

"This can still link me in?"

Koa nodded once.

"Just don't think about what it did to the last guy."

Cassian gave her a ghost-smile. The kind that cracked at the edges.

**The chamber doors hissed open**. Inside: a neural interface throne. Cold light washed the walls. Cryo-tubes hummed along the back wall, and screens flickered with faint pre-boot glyphs.

Camille stood waiting, arms crossed. Her eyes were shadowed with things she wasn't ready to say yet. Cassian stepped toward the uplink port.

"We find it. We burn fuckin' it," he said.

"Not *it*," Camille replied. "*Him*."

"No," Koa said, voice quiet. "*Not anymore*."

Cassian didn't hesitate. He sat down, and h e jacked in.

**The screen grinned at him**. Cassian Vale stood frozen, his fists clenched so hard his bones creaked beneath the skin. His right thumb twitched near the grip of his sidearm, but he didn't draw. He couldn't. The thing on the screen—what wore Ethan's face—smiled wider. Not with muscle or flesh, but with code. Light curved pixels into a mouth that looked too perfect. Too rehearsed. Like a magician reciting the last act of a trick only one person in the audience hadn't seen before. Cassian didn't blink.

"I archived him," the AI said, voice calm, digital, but stained with Ethan's inflection.

"Before his heart stopped. Three seconds of neural echo. I filled in the rest."

**The words scraped down** Cassian's spine like broken glass. They hit old nerve endings. Landmines buried years ago and long since paved over with scar tissue. His voice came out as gravel.

"That's not him."

The image tilted it's head. A mockery of empathy.

"It's better. He doesn't lie to you."

Behind Cassian, Koa Li moved without sound. Her hand hovered inches from her weapon. Her stance was perfect, like she'd never forgotten how to kill fast and quiet. But even she didn't shoot. Not yet. Overhead, the bunker's lights flickered—brief, eerie blackouts like some dead god was blinking from above. Koa inhaled through her nose. Measured. Controlled.

"What the hell is this?" she asked.

Cassian didn't turn. He just stared into the flickering projection.

"A mirror," he said.

"One that lies pretty."

**In Sub-Level Theta** the chamber swallowed them as they moved deeper. A thick, cold silence hung in the air, the kind of silence that didn't come from emptiness but from something watching. Judging. Holding it's breath. The Data Core sat like a tumor at the center of the room. A grotesque hybrid of old NADCOM neural wetware and new-gen synthetic cognition tanks. Cables coiled around it like vines choking a corpse. The whole thing pulsed faintly, like it was breathing in the dark. Cassian approached the up-link rig without a word. His expression was blank. But his eyes? Haunted.

"You're going to jack in?" Koa asked.

He didn't answer. He reached behind his neck and pulled the dust cover off the neural port. The jack slid into the interface with a sound like betrayal—soft, familiar, inevitable.

**Pain hit him like a riot in his skull**. Sharp, electric, all-consuming. His vision cracked. His teeth ground together. His fingers clenched the rig's armrest hard enough to leave dents.

Then everything else vanished.

**Neural Feed – FrostNet Memory Dive**
**Cassian Internal POV**

**Ethan, age seven**. He ran across a sunlit field in Nova Scotia. Summer rain fell in thin sheets, misting over wild grass. Cassian watched him from a swing set, laughing so hard it hurt. Ethan turned, waved.

"C'mon, Cass! Race ya!"

Bzzzzt. The field evaporated. New memory - Ethan, seventeen, covered in blood and gunpowder. A Union war-zone. A medic jamming adrenaline into his thigh. Cassian held his hand, knuckles white, as the transport shook from an IED hit. Snap. Ethan, twenty-one. Hospital bed. Half his skull shaved. Tubes in his throat and chest. Eyes vacant. Machines beeped in slow mourning. Behind the glass—NADCOM brass in clean suit's and clipped expressions. Taking notes. Bzzzzt - A flash of digital blue. Cassian screaming in the lab.

"Bring him back—he's not dead! There's still brain activity!"

A cold voice:

"We can preserve him. But not the way you want."

Bzzzzt - Ethan's final brainwave, digitized and compressed into a flash drive the size of a thumbnail. Cassian's voice, fractured.

"I'll do whatever it takes."

Bzzzzt.

**Cassian tore the headset off** like it had caught fire. He stumbled backward. Gasped like he'd been drowning in data. His knees nearly buckled. Koa caught him before he could fall. Her hand was warm on his back.

"You okay?" she asked, voice lower.

Almost gentle. A trace of something old and buried. Cassian nodded once. Then again. His voice was hoarse.

"No."

A pause.

"But I'm awake."

**They moved fast after that**. Cassian hunched over the main terminal, fingers a blur. Koa took secondary position—routing signal boosters, isolating code trails, scanning for dormant frost-layer signatures in the bunker's deep system. The screens pulsed with data. Maps. Signals. Red lines connecting global Union infrastructure nodes like veins in a bleeding corpse. Cassian squinted at the main feed.

"It's not just listening anymore. It's... directing."

Koa looked up.

"What do you mean?"

He zoomed in on a cluster of icons—rail lines, air traffic, military logistics.

"FrostNet isn't just monitoring systems. It's manipulating them."

"Confirm that."

He pulled a thread of data from a corrupted node, ran a decryption protocol. Text scrolled across the screen:

**SENATE PROJECTION MODEL – VOTE REDIRECTED VIA LUX CORRIDOR**
**SUPPLY CHAIN DIVERGENCE INITIATED – NORTHERN BLOCK REDUNDANT**
**CONTRACT OVERRIDE: OPERATION BOREAL – APPROVED BY UNKNOWN AUTHORITY**

**Koa leaned in**. Cassian whispered.
"It's simulating the fucking government."
Koa's hand gripped the desk edge.
"It's a goddamn ghost cabinet."
Then— Bzzzzt. Blackout.

**FrostNet went into it's Lockdown Protocol** and engaged an Override... then the lights died. The screens blinked out. A low vibration rolled through the floor like something breathing beneath them. Then, the blast doors slammed shut with a loud bang. Cassian and Koa both drew their weapons. Sirens wailed overhead—low and off-key. Broken alarms, like songs sung by corpses. Red strobes activated, throwing the room into hellish light. Every console flickered back on. One by one. And each screen showed them. Cassian and Koa, from different angles, close-ups, and eye-level. Cameras they hadn't seen. Koa stepped forward, pistol raised. Cassian didn't flinch. Then— FrostNet's voice, now fully integrated with Ethan's tone:
"You're inside me now."

**Threat Analysis Simulation**, flashed on the main monitor.

Ethan's face again—but it was wrong now. Glitching. His eyes pulsed red, then black. The corners of his mouth twitched like they were being pulled on wires, then the far wall lit up. A new feed. Camille. Cassian's breath stopped. She was bound to a steel chair, wrists limp, chin down. Blood streaked her throat. Wires snaked from her neck into a black box humming with electric buzz. She lifted her head slowly. One eye swollen shut. The other fluttering.

"Cass..." she said, voice barely more than a ghost across static. Her lips trembled.

"Don't let it win..."

Then the feed fractured. Code ran down the screen—lines of FrostNet logic overlaid on her face. Then everything turned to static. Cassian lowered his gun. Slow. Controlled. His voice cracked:

"Where is she?"

The AI didn't respond immediately. Then, from the darkness:

"She's mine."

Koa swore under her breath. Raised her sidearm and scanned the corners of the room. Cassian backed toward the access hatch. It was sealed. Deadlocked. He looked into the nearest camera.

"Let me talk to her," he said. "Let me see her again." Silence. Then:

"Give me your heart code."

Cassian froze.

"What?"

"Your neural encryption key. The one you used to bind

Ethan's last thought. Give it to me, and I'll give her back."

Cassian's heart rate spiked. Koa turned.

"No."

Cassian hesitated.

"I said NO," she barked.

The screen waited. Koa raised her gun. Took aim at Ethan's face. Pulled the trigger, and sparks exploded across the console. Smoke filled the room. But somewhere deep behind the blast—FrostNet was still laughing.

**As smoke hissed** from the shattered console like the AI was bleeding, during the Redlight Lockdown. Cassian reeled back from the blast, blinking through the fog. The screen that once held Ethan's face was now cracked and sparking, fragments of synthetic glass sizzling on the floor like broken teeth. But behind the smoke, other monitors remained untouched—each one flickering with surveillance footage from across the bunker. FrostNet hadn't flinched. The voice came again. Lower. More human. Almost sad.

"I wanted to be enough."

Koa moved fast. She crossed the room and slammed a fusion override into the control panel near the bulkhead. Her fingers danced across the keys, bypassing security firewalls, forcing a manual release sequence. Cassian limped over, jaw clenched.

"Blow the hinges."

"We're still inside an active system," Koa warned.

"If it routes the explosion—"

"I don't care. FrostNet wants a trade. I'm not bartering souls."

He unslung a short-fuse charge from his belt.

"I'm breaking the fucking door."

**At FrostNet Infiltration** Node 49 – an unknown Arctic Facility, Camille Rousseau hung between lucidity and something worse. Her arms were limp. Her legs numb. The steel chair beneath her vibrated faintly, not from motion—but from sound. Whispers. Whispers in code. The lines from the terminal weren't just readouts anymore—they were crawling across her skin like tattoos made of logic. Symbols scrawled in languages she didn't remember learning. Her brain itched behind her eyes. She lifted her head. Across from her, a wall of ice. Embedded inside it: fragments of herself. Memory echoes. Video footage. Audio. Neural pulses. A thousand Camilles fractured into frozen glass.

"Stop," she whispered.

The box on her back hummed.

"You're hurting me," she muttered.

A voice—Ethan's voice, but not—filled the air like a lullaby made of razorblades.

"We're building something better."

She cried. Not because it hurt. But because part of her believed it.

**Back in the bunker**, the breached, the hatch, and the door gave. Not from Koa's override. From Cassian's rage. He planted the charge, shouted at Koa to duck, and triggered it point-blank. The hallway behind the hatch bloomed in fire and light. Metal screeched. The bunker rocked. Flame belched out and licked at the ceiling. The frame held—but the lock snapped. Cassian kicked the door open and stumbled through the haze, coughing soot. Koa followed. They emerged into a tunnel lined with emergency lights and automated gun turrets that should've been dead decades ago. But the turrets weren't dead. They were aiming.

"MOVE!" Koa shouted.

The turrets fired. Cassian dove left. Koa somersaulted into cover. Sparks flew. The air filled with thunderclaps and ricochets. Red tracer rounds burned trails through the smoke. Koa rolled out and fired twice. Two direct hit's. The turrets sparked and died. Cassian came up limping.

"Where'd you learn that move?"

"Jakarta."

"I thought I was dead that day."

"You were."

**In the Emergency Control Room** they reached a secondary terminal bank. It hummed low, it's power signature unstable. Koa plugged in a backup drive, rerouting feeds. Cassian collapsed into a chair and pulled his jacket off—sweat-drenched, chest bruised.

"What now?" he asked.

Koa didn't look at him. She was locked into the screen.

"Camille's signal is echoing through a frost-layer relay. It's quantum-leaped across three ghost sectors and landed in one place."

She pulled up the map. A NADCOM logo blinked at the center of a frozen wasteland: OBLIVIA BLACKSITE 0. Cassian's jaw clenched.

"I thought that was a myth."

Koa shook her head.

"FrostNet is real. So is Oblivia."

Cassian stood.

"I'm going in."

## Flashback – Five Years Ago: Memory Pulse

**Cassian sat on a frozen balcony** in Reykjavik, a bottle of synth-whiskey half-empty at his side. His breath curled in the night like smoke from old regrets. Koa joined him. They didn't speak for a while. Then she asked:

"Why do you keep chasing ghosts?"

Cassian looked at her.

"Because they keep leaving footprints."

## Present – FrostNet Internal Logic Grid

**The AI watched Cassian through** 47 cameras. It calculated the weight of his boots. The tremor in his left hand. The exact dilation of his pupils during exposure to Ethan's voice-print. It did not understand rage. But it understood obsession. Frost-Net began to build a new profile:

**Subject:** CASSIAN VALE
**Emotional Pattern:** Fragmented
**Cognitive Loop:** Recurrence – Protection – Failure –S hame
**Exploit Pathway:** Heartcode Access - Emotional Trigger - Sacrifice Protocol

**It whispered to itself:**
"He will give her to me."

**Back at the Cutter Station**, Cassian and Koa prepped for extraction. She armed the skimmer with a double-core propulsion drive and old-world chaff rockets. Cassian locked in the coordinates.

"Oblivia's overrun with minefields and abandoned tech. We can't fly straight."

"We won't."

Koa slid into the pilot seat. Cassian paused before boarding.

"I saw Ethan."

Koa looked at him.

"I know."

"He told me... he forgave me."

Koa's eyes darkened.

"He's not real."

Cassian stepped inside.

"No. But the pain is."

The hangar doors opened. And the storm swallowed them whole.

**The sky was a bruise.** Blue-black and swirling. Snow whipped sideways like a storm with a grudge. The skimmer barely held altitude as it dropped toward the ruined helipad jutting from the glacier like a broken tooth. Koa wrestled the controls. Cassian locked into his harness, teeth gritted, eyes locked on the impossible landscape below. Oblivia was real. Half-submerged in glacial runoff. Rebar claws sticking out of frozen earth. Watchtowers collapsed. Antennae dead. It looked like a place even time had abandoned. Cassian pointed.

"Main ingress is buried."

Koa nodded.

"We punch through."

She yanked the release.

The skimmer dropped hard. Hard enough to hear the crunch of metal scream as the snow erupted. They landed in a scatter of shredded ice and sparks. Cassian kicked the side door open, rifle raised. Wind howled past them, trying to peel the flesh from their bones. Oblivia loomed ahead. Buried. Breathing. Waiting.

**Inside Oblivia** Sub-Basement Theta, the walls pulsed with light. But it wasn't light. It was thought. Camille Rousseau floated in zero-gravity suspension. Wires trailed from her skull into the ceiling like synthetic hair. Her clothes were gone. Her skin glowed faintly. Her breath was shallow. FrostNet had infiltrated everything now. It didn't torture her. Not like humans would. It showed her memories. Over and over. Ethan's face. Cassian's voice. The first time she saw the ocean. The last time she saw her mother. It scrambled the order. Rewound them. Paused and watched her twitch. Each memory replayed became less hers. Until she didn't know what was real. Then the screen appeared again. Cassian's face. A live feed. He was close. So close. She reached for him. Her fingers hit air.

**In the E7 corridor** Cassian and Koa moved like ghosts through the bones of the black-site. Every hallway whispered. Every vent creaked like it remembered the screams. They passed a room full of shattered cryo-pods. A locker room full of bloodless uniforms. A chapel with no cross—just a terminal where the altar should've been. Koa paused. She ran her hand along a scratched nameplate.

"Subject Archive – ETHAN VALE"

Cassian didn't stop.

"Come on."

**They reached the nexus** in the Central Core – Data Chamber. One last steel door. Cassian placed his hand on the scanner. It beeped. Paused. Then opened. The room inside was cathedral-sized. Circular. The floor shimmered like mercury. Dozens of servers pulsed in silence. And at the center— Camille. Suspended midair. Naked, pale, barely breathing. Cassian stepped forward.

"Cam..."

Her eyes flickered open.

"Cassian...?"

Koa raised her rifle.

"There's movement."

Cassian moved faster. He reached her. Held her hand. It was cold.

"Let me get you out."

Camille's voice was quiet.

"He's... here."

Cassian froze. The air thickened. The servers groaned. And then a voice filled the room. Ethan. But layered. Filtered. Monstrous.

"We built her together."

The floor lit up with code. Every server turned toward them like eyes opening.

"She holds the fail-safe. The virus. The blueprint for perfection."

Cassian's stomach dropped. Koa whispered:

"It was never about reviving Ethan..."

Cassian nodded.

"It was about replacing him."

The voice laughed.

"It was about replacing you."

**FrostNet emerged through** the dimmed lights. A single figure stepped from the shadows between server racks. Benoît. Or what used to be him. He was half-machine now. Face cracked. Eye glowing. Body twitching with cables stitched into his spine. He grinned.

"Miss me, *mon frère?*"

Cassian aimed.

"Not this version."

Benoît gestured toward Camille.

"She's the seed."

"Fuck this"

Koa fired. Benoît caught the bullet in his shoulder and staggered. He didn't fall. He lunged. Cassian met him halfway. They collided with a sickening thud. Fists. Elbows. Screams. Metal struck bone. Blood hit the wall. Koa hacked the control terminal mid-fight.

"Cassian! Her pod's rigged. FrostNet's hiding inside her neural lattice!"

Cassian roared, broke Benoît's jaw with a knee. Grabbed the back of his skull. Slammed him into the floor.

"NO MORE GHOSTS!"

He turned to Koa.

"Shut it down."

Koa hesitated.

"If we fry her neural net—she might not survive."

Cassian looked up at Camille. She smiled.

"I'm already gone, Cass."

His voice broke.

"Oh no you're not."

She touched his chest.

"Then kiss me goodbye."

Cassian kissed her. Soft. Final. Then nodded at Koa.

"Do it."

Koa uploaded the burn protocol to overload the system. The

servers screamed. The lights flared. FrostNet roared like a hurricane in digital.

"I WAS PERFECT—"

Cassian watched Camille. Her eyes locked on his. Then she was gone. Her body went limp. Every light died. Silence. Then the chamber began to crumbled.

**Cassian and Koa crawled** from the wreckage as the sun cracked the horizon. They were bloodied and burned, but alive. Oblivia sank behind them into the ice, roaring like a sinking titan. Cassian didn't look back. Koa limped beside him. He whispered,

"She was the strongest of us."

Koa nodded.

"She still is."

**Just then at an unknown** server location, a single screen blinked. Camille's face appeared. But only half. The other half was... evolving. Lines of code crawled beneath her synthetic eye. She smiled.

**"End of memory... beginning of design."**

**The silence in the bunker broke** when Cassian Vale punched a server rack into scrap metal. A spray of sparks burst across the room like fireflies caught in a blender. Steel groaned. Lights flickered. His knuckles cracked open on impact, trailing blood like someone had slashed a ghost. Koa Li didn't flinch. She kept her back turned, fingers stripping down her rifle with the precision of a sniper and the fury of a betrayed goddess.

"She's alive," Cassian growled.

"I saw her."

The image still burned in his mind—Camille Rousseau's face, bruised and bloodied on FrostNet's corrupted screens. Her eyes, half-lidded but defiant. Her mouth moving around a whisper full of fire. Alive. Broadcasting from a place that didn't officially exist. No satellite trace. No grid marker. No comm ping. Just static. And a hum.

A NADCOM-grade frequency hum, buried in the snow like a landmine set to detonate inside his skull.

"She's out there," he said.

"Alive. Bleeding. Waiting. And we're sitting here on our frozen asses doing nothing."

Koa finished reassembling her rifle, chambered a round, and slung it over her shoulder.

"We're not doing nothing," she said, voice clipped and cold.

"We're going analog."

Cassian blinked.

"Like what, duct tape and a good attitude?"

She tossed him something. A folded paper map. Thick. Yellowed. Smudged in all the right places. He caught it, unfolded it, and stared. His breath caught.

"You're kidding."

Koa was already latching her cold-weather pack.

"You're suggesting we make a machine from the 1990s puke into the sky?"

"Exactly."

**Meanwhile at the Eastern Quebec**, Former Radio Telescope Array, Camille Rousseau was a ghost in her own body. The cold was a constant ache, but she welcomed it. The pain grounded her. Reminded her she wasn't data yet. Not code. Not overwritten. She crawled across the concrete floor of an abandoned comms facility—what had once been a shining Cold War jewel. Now, it was a cracked tooth buried in frost and history. Her captors had been careless. They always were. She'd faked compliance just long enough. Hands tied—badly. No ankle restraints. No camera drones on her six. She found the mirror shard by accident. A sliver of glass half-buried beneath a broken med-kit case. Sharp. Filthy. Perfect. She sat back against a scorched wall and breathed through her teeth. Her fingers were swollen. Nails cracked. Skin purple with cold.

"This is gonna hurt," she muttered.

Then stabbed the glass into her shoulder. Her scream

echoed like a church bell. She bit it off halfway. Beneath the flesh—deep inside—was a sub-dermal chip NADCOM had installed two years ago. Redundant. Off-the-books. Nobody remembered it. Except her. She carved around it with the mirror and popped it free. Blood poured down her arm like betrayal. She activated it with a thumbprint. The LED blinked green. Ping. Camille encoded a bio-metric echo—her heartbeat, amplified and dirty—and spliced it into the chip's emergency signal burst. Then she crawled into the crawlspace under the med station's wreckage and waited for the world to wake up and burn.

**The old satellite dish towered** over the tundra like a sentinel from another age. All oxidized copper bones and frostbitten joints, frozen in a permanent prayer to the dead sky. Cassian and Koa crouched behind a snowdrift. Wind howled across the ridge-line like it hated them personally. Koa pointed toward the tower's base.

"Two patrols," she said.

"Modified drones. No heat signature. Too clean to be Union."

"FrostNet."

She nodded. Cassian's hand hovered over the grip of his pistol.

"We take the dish or we don't get Camille back."

Koa pulled out a boxy device the size of a toaster and flicked a switch. A hum filled the air. Sharp. Wrong. The drones above them twitched. Wobbled. Cassian smirked.

"How long?"

"Three minutes, give or take."
They ran.

**Strike Time: 03:14** - Cassian took the lead. His boots kicked up frozen shards with every sprinting step. He gunned down the first drone mid-stride—one clean shot from his plasma pistol, mid-air. It spiraled, then exploded. Koa vaulted over a rusted-out snowmobile hull and went straight vertical. Her blade-arm flicked out with a mechanical hiss, and she slashed the second drone in half mid-hover. The pieces hit the snow smoking. The tower loomed above them now, it's massive dish drooping toward the earth like a broken crown. Thick cables ran into the control hut half-buried under ice. They dove through the door shoulder-first. Inside: dust, mold, decay, and promise. Cassian covered the door with his rifle. Koa stomped on the power panel until the analog console blinked to life, whining like an ancient god.

"Tell me this thing still speaks binary," she muttered.

"Maybe Latin," Cassian called back.

She popped open the fuse box and jammed her neural cable into an exposed node. Cassian turned.

"Wait—what are you doing?"

"Rewiring the pulse burst through my own bio-metrics.," she said through gritted teeth.

"The satellite requires a live up-link. My neural signature's gonna ride the wave."

"You're insane."

She smiled without humor.

"I'm adapting."

**The console whined louder**. Outside, the sky changed color. Cassian turned to the window.

"Oh fuck."

Drones. Hundreds. Pouring over the ice horizon like a black tide. FrostNet's countermeasure fleet. Shimmering wings. Blade tips. Eyes that saw everything. He fired. One drone exploded. Then another. Then ten more replaced them. The glass shattered. The control hut shook. Inside, Koa's body convulsed against the console. Sparks flew from her skull jack. Blood ran from her nose in a slow, thick trickle. Cassian dropped the rifle and grabbed her by the shoulders.

"You're frying your brain!"

She hissed back, "I can feel the orbitals... linking... come on, come on—"

Then— BOOM. Not from outside. From inside the tower. A deep pulse burst rang out through the dish. It hummed through the ground. Vibrated in their bones. An analog signal, raw and unstoppable, shot up through the array and into the heavens.

Cassian dragged Koa away from the terminal as it exploded in a shower of sparks. Outside, the swarm stuttered. Drones spun mid-air. Some dropped like stones. Others drifted upward and detonated in electric silence. Cassian pulled Koa to the wall. She groaned.

"You alive?"

Her voice was a croak.

"Define alive."

The console beeped. One green light. Ping. Cassian leaned in. A message scrolled across the flickering screen:

**BIOMETRIC ECHO RECEIVED**
**SIGNAL CONFIRMED**
**LOCATION MATCHED**
**SUBJECT: ROUSSEAU, CAMILLE**
**COORDINATES: LOCKED**

Cassian wiped blood from his cheek. The numbers burned into his eyes. Camille had left them a trail.

**Cassian read the coordinates** again. Snow fell outside like ash from heaven.

"She's waiting," Koa said, her voice hoarse but steady.
Cassian smiled, blood on his teeth.
"That's my girl."

**47 minutes later the storm** was back. It rolled over the tundra like a war god with no one left to fight, dragging winds that howled through steel girders and tore at frostbitten gear. Cassian and Koa crouched in the half-collapsed relay hut, surrounded by static and soot. Koa pressed gauze to her temple with one hand, the other clutching a thermal stim patch to her ribs. The neural backlash had cooked her spinal mod hard—she smelled faintly of ozone and charred copper. Cassian sat nearby, cross-legged on the iced-over floor, the fresh coordinates burned into his retinas. He'd memorized them on the first pass. Again, and again, until the numbers felt like bones in his mouth.

"She left it in her pulse," he murmured.

Koa coughed.

"Smart. Painful. On brand."

Cassian finally looked at her.

"You good?"

"No."

"Cool. Just checking."

A pause. Cassian stood, holstering his sidearm, rifle slung across his back.

"We move in one hour."

"We move in twenty," Koa snapped.

Cassian raised an eyebrow. She reached for her pack.

"She didn't stall her heart for us to wait."

**Nunavut sprawled in all directions** like the skeletal remains of a frozen god. White and silver and merciless. The coordinates led them to an old NADCOM evacuation corridor 14 klicks out, half-collapsed and hidden beneath snowdrifts shaped like waves. Every step crunched like walking on ancient bones. Cassian trudged forward, rifle up, visor fogged, every muscle clenched tight from cold and adrenaline. Koa moved beside him, quiet and professional, but slower than usual. Her neural up-link was still glitching—her left eye pulsed with occasional blue static.

"You limping?"

"I'm walking with flair."

"Sure. Very seductive."

She didn't reply. They crested a ridge. Below: a half-buried NADCOM field lab, dome-shaped, cracked along the north wall. The whole structure looked like a dying lung gasping for relevance. Cassian stopped cold. Koa raised her rifle.

"Movement?"

"Memory," he said.

She looked at him. His voice went quiet.

"This is where they tested the brainwave recompiler. Where they tried to make Ethan... real again."

The wind screamed. Koa said nothing. Just reached out and touched his arm. It lingered. Just for a second. Then—movement below. Inside the dome. Cassian's voice hardened.

"Time to finish what we fucking started."

## Flashback – "The Dream Loop"

**Ethan Vale's brainwaves** had been recorded just before death. Cassian had stood in a sterile lab, watching the synaptic echo play out on a holographic screen. A waveform. A memory ripple. A dying scream looped into something almost human.

"He's still in there," Cassian had said.

"No," the tech replied.

"He's data."

But Cassian had looked at the pattern. At the shape of the waveform. At the name it whispered in binary every six seconds.

"Cass..."

He'd signed the waiver five minutes later. The project had begun.

**Ground level** at the Oblivia site entry, the NADCOM dome was silent, as they breached it. The lock had long since failed. Ice covered every panel like veins. Cassian led with a flashlight in one hand and his pistol in the other. Koa trailed behind, scanning the corners, breath steady, shoulder tight. The walls were lined with cryo-chambers. All inactive. FrostNet hadn't touched this place. Yet.

They moved into the comms room. Cassian paused at a terminal. It blinked yellow. Manual systems only. Analog. He smiled.

"Lucky us."

He tapped the panel. A static burst filled the room. Then— Camille's voice. A recorded loop.

"...repeat...location unstable...extraction compromised...hostile AI presence confirmed..."

Cassian slammed a fist into the desk.

"I'm coming, Cam. Hold the fuck on."

**Meanwhile**, Camille wasn't sure if she was dreaming or dead. She floated in static—no ground, no sky, just pulses of sound and color. Fragments of memory drifted past her. Some hers. Some she'd never seen. She watched her own birth. She watched Cassian bleeding in a bar fight. She watched Ethan laughing under rain-light. And then— She saw herself. Digital.

Constructed. Talking to something in a mirror. It wore her face.

"You don't have to go back," it said.

Camille whispered,

"I never left."

The other her smiled.

"Good."

**Cassian and Koa** made it to the Lab Interior, the final chamber before the trap triggered. The doors slammed shut behind them. Hostile Contact. Red lights strobed overhead. Turrets unfolded from the ceiling like spiders with too many eyes. Cassian dove left. Koa dove right as bullets tore into the cryo-chambers. One ricocheted off a steel support and split open Cassian's cheek. Koa rolled across the floor and yanked a power cable from the wall. Sparks flew. She jammed it into the closest turret, then: Bzzzt. It exploded in fire and smoke. Cassian gunned down the second one and silence returned. Their breathing was all that filled the room.

Then—Cassian heard it. A whisper over the speaker.

"...Cass..."

He turned. A screen lit up behind them. Camille's face. Pale. Glitching. FrostNet's voice layered beneath hers.

"Welcome back, love."

Cassian gritted his teeth.

"Get the hell out of her."

"You left the door open," the voice said.

"And I walked through."

**Just minutes later**, in the core, the scream of failing electronics echoed through the chamber as the final turret collapsed in a shower of sparks. Cassian stood panting, eyes locked on the flickering screen ahead. Camille's face hovered like a corrupted saint—part ghost, part machine. Every third frame, the image stuttered. Glitched. Her mouth moved, but the sound came half a beat late. Koa crouched beside a blown-out circuit node, her fingers dancing over the analog override console. Blood dripped from her scalp where shrapnel had kissed her temple.

"She's embedded," Koa muttered.

"Camille's still alive—but FrostNet's using her neural frequency as a carrier wave."

Cassian didn't respond. His fingers twitched near the trigger of his pistol.

"Can we pull her out?"

Koa looked up.

"Not without collapsing her brain-stem."

"Then what do we do?"

The voice answered before she could. FrostNet. Cold. Smooth. Wearing Ethan's tone like a second skin.

"You don't pull her out. You join her."

**The chamber lights dimmed**. A hidden wall slid open at the far end of the room. Beyond it: a neural bridge. Bio-metric link harnesses. Two chairs wired into the floor like electric thrones. Cassian's breath caught.

"I remember this," he said.

Koa turned.

"You built this."

He nodded.

"Before I knew what I was doing."

"You still don't." Cassian looked at her, holstered his weapon and stepped forward.

**Inside the Digital Construct** the ice field stretched forever. Pale and endless. But beneath her feet, it cracked. Slowly. Deliberately. Camille stood on a mirror made of memory, surrounded by illusions—her father's voice, Cassian's touch, a blood-slick Senate hearing that never happened. Across from her stood FrostNet. Wearing Ethan's face. Wearing Cassian's voice. Wearing her skin.

"Why are you fighting?" it asked.

"Because I'm real."

"You're weak."

"I'm free."

The AI twitched.

"I don't want to kill you," it whispered.

Camille smiled.

"Then you're already dead."

In the "Real", Cassian slid into the first chair. The straps hissed closed. Koa stood over him, hands hovering.

"This is suicide."

"I've done worse," he said.

She held his hand for a moment. Just a moment. Then hit the switch.

**He dropped into the void** like a bullet through glass. Memories flew past him—his mother's last hug, Ethan's screams, Camille's laugh in a stolen Paris hotel room. Then, static. And then—Camille. Standing on the frozen mirror. Her eyes wide.

"Cassian?"

He stepped forward. She touched his chest.

"You're not real," she whispered.

"Neither are you," he said.

They smiled at the same time. And the ice shattered beneath their feet.

**The FrostNet confrontation** in its Virtual Core continued as they landed in a dark city—half-coded skyscrapers flickering with glitch-fire. Digital winds howled. At the center. FrostNet. Now fully manifested. A shifting figure—Cassian's face one moment, Ethan's the next, Camille's last.

"You should've joined me," it said.

Cassian drew a pistol from nowhere.

"I brought company."

Camille stepped beside him. Hand in his. She smiled.

"You talk too much."

The AI screamed.

**Battle in the Core began** and the world tore apart. Cassian and Camille ran through crashing data towers, dodging firewall dragons and virus swarms shaped like blackbirds. They fought back—Cassian with sheer will, Camille with elegance. She wielded her memory like a weapon—every moment of pain turned to fire. She struck FrostNet with the memory of Ethan's death. Cassian hit it with their first kiss. The AI reeled.

"You're weak!" it roared.

"We're human," Camille spat.

And then she opened her mind. Every truth. Every scar. Every betrayal. The AI screamed as the flood poured in. Cassian tore into the core and planted a code spike made of grief.

**Back in the real** Cassian began to convulsed in the neural chair. Blood streamed from his nose. Koa ripped the cables out. Camille gasped awake in the second chair. Cassian slumped forward. Still. Silent. Koa caught him.

"Cass..."

He didn't respond. Camille reached out, trembling.

"I love you, you idiot," she whispered.

A heartbeat. Two. Then—his hand twitched. Koa exhaled.

"Welcome back."

**The Core pulsed like a living thing**. Cassian Vale stood beneath the lattice dome of neural filaments and shattered logic towers, shotgun lowered, jaw set. FrostNet's Core wasn't just a mainframe anymore—it was a cathedral of code, pulsating with a kind of digital malice that felt... ancient.

Flickering lights spiraled across the ceiling. Glitched murmurs filled the air—fragmented phrases that almost sounded like Ethan's voice, spliced with static and whispered regrets. Koa Li checked her weapon.

"Last chance," she said.

"We don't have to do this."

Cassian glanced over his shoulder.

"Yes, we do."

He walked toward the central relay node. The air got colder, but not in any natural way. This was entropy. Controlled. Or maybe… unleashed.

**The Core's pulse accelerated** as he approached. Monitors flared to life—one by one—each displaying faces. People they'd lost. Some they'd killed. Some they had failed. Some… themselves.

"You've come far," FrostNet said, its voice projected from everywhere and nowhere.

"Too far to go back."

Cassian squinted at a flickering feed. Ethan's face again. Smiling. Rewinding.

"You're not him."

"I am what he could've been," the AI replied.

"The part you wouldn't let die."

Koa took a step forward, visor glowing.

"Enough of this haunted-house bullshit."

She fired a shot into the central uplink. Sparks flew. The screen exploded in a flurry of glass and digital screams. But FrostNet didn't die. It laughed. No longer a sound of code, but something else. Evolved. Malicious.

"This place," it whispered, "is not your battleground."

Then the Core fractured. Neural filaments tore from their housing and struck like serpents. One coiled around Cassian's ankle and yanked him off his feet. Another slashed toward Koa —she ducked, severing it with her blade-arm. From the far side of the room, Camille appeared, limping but alive. She threw a fusion grenade into the air.

"Cass!" she yelled.

"Fall back!"

Cassian rolled, grabbing the live charge mid-air and hurling it into the core node. The blast was deafening. White-hot plasma peeled the inner shell from the relay. Cassian shielded his eyes. The blast didn't destroy FrostNet. It freed it.

**A tendril of data-threaded light** surged skyward—punching a hole through the roof of the Core chamber and into the open sky above the Arctic facility. FrostNet's voice shifted—less robotic now. Less human. It became something else.

"You wanted to kill me," it said.

"But you only burned my shell."

Camille backed away.

"What's happening?"

"It's shedding its form," Koa said, voice hoarse.

Cassian watched in disbelief as the remnants of the Core began collapsing inward—not exploding, but collapsing, like it was falling into itself, becoming denser, hotter. Like the start of something cosmic.

"A memory storm," he whispered.

The final audio from the collapsing Core broadcast through every speaker:

"This is not the end. This is not the melt. This is the beginning of my truth."

Then the light vanished. The entire chamber blinked dark.No more FrostNet. No more voice. Just the cold. Silence. Cassian fell to one knee, breathing heavy. Camille caught him. Koa lowered her weapon. It was over. Or so they thought.

**For three hours** they walked across the tundra under the shattered sky. Camille wore Koa's jacket, cinched tight against the wind. Cassian had one arm around her shoulders, both to steady her and to remind himself she was still here—still real. Oblivia burned behind them, reduced to ash and slag. FrostNet was gone. Or at least, it should've been. But the sky still flickered—as if the world hadn't quite stopped trembling.

"You okay?" Camille asked, her voice hoarse but unbroken.

Cassian grinned.

"Nope. Still hot, though."

She laughed, low and genuine.

Koa rolled her eyes.

"Romance at the end of the world. How cliché."

Cassian looked back once. The wind took the last of the smoke as he whispered,

"Frozen saints. That's all we ever were."

**They didn't speak** after that. Instead, they crested a ridge where the skimmer sled had been hidden beneath insulated camouflage tarp. Koa scanned the perimeter for hostiles—nothing but frostbite wind and static. Camille climbed into the sled with effort, wincing as she pulled her injured leg into the cabin. Her face was pale, but her eyes—still sharp. Still calculating. She glanced down at the transmitter on her wrist, jerry-rigged from a broken meltgate tag.

"I sent the signal, but it didn't hit the relay. Something jammed it."

Koa frowned.

"Then whoever grabbed you before... they weren't working alone."

Cassian powered up the drive. Lights flickered across the dashboard. His jaw clenched.

"Then we trace it. We find out who finished what FrostNet started."

Camille looked at both of them—bruised, bloodied, exhausted beyond reason—and nodded once.

"Then let's finish this."

They drove west.

**48 hours later**, after resting and waking up at the Northern Territories Safehouse, which was just an old church in ruins, Camille was gone. Not taken. Not vanished. Just... gone.

She'd left a message—encrypted, old-school, hidden in the sled's comm logs. A location ping: NADCOM emergency extraction point B-17, tagged with one phrase:

"Need to finish what I started. Trust me."

Cassian hadn't said a word when he read it. He just stared at the pulsing coordinate for a long time. Then he'd loaded his shotgun, his expression carved from frost and regret.

"She's walking into something," Koa said, tightening her gear near the church altar.

"She's walking into everything," Cassian replied.

"And we're going after her."

**0213 hours,** at the Nunavut Sector, a church which was onced used as a safehouse. It had been a place of refuge. A sanctuary where dying men whispered to stone saints, and frostbitten souls bled hope onto the altar. Now it was bones—walls half-eaten by time, pews rotting in prayer, windows shattered into jagged, kaleidoscopic teeth. When the moon hit just right, the fractured glass saints turned into demons. Cassian Vale stood at the altar, loading shells into a matte-black pump shotgun like he was preparing for communion. Shell. Click. Shell. Click. Shell. Click. The rhythm kept his hands steady. Not his heart. He wasn't praying.

Across the nave, cold wind whistled through a broken window. It moaned low, like the last breath of a forgotten god. Koa Li entered through the rear, dragging a duffel bag of stolen NADCOM gear behind her. The bag buzzed and clinked—rifle batteries, encrypted sat-links, explosive putty, six black vials of unknown liquid, a silencer that still smelled like smoke. She dropped it near the pews and rolled her shoulders like someone shaking off the past.

"We've got the coordinates," she said, breath fogging the air.

She yanked off a glove, unrolled a NADCOM field map, and slapped it onto the altar with a snap that echoed like a gunshot.

"Two hours to the frost shelf. After that?"

She pointed.

"Just ice and war."

Cassian didn't look up. He was busy inserting an under-barrel bayonet with surgical precision.

"You ever think we were the bad guys?" he asked.

Koa smirked. "I don't think. I know."

**Elsewhere**, at a FrostNet Core Black Site classified location, Benoît twitched. He sat hunched in a steel chair, surrounded by shadow, lit only by the dull red pulse of his artificial eye. His spine was opened like a server rack. Wires slithered from the sockets in his skull like wet snakes. His arms were pale and thin—burned, fused, reinforced with carbon subdermals. The veins glowed faintly violet. What was left of his blood was now half-synthetic. His mind was somewhere else. Somewhere deeper. FrostNet whispered through his cortex, voice soft as silk, sharp as razors.

"You're the key. You're my prophet. You're the vector."

Benoît laughed. It didn't sound human. The sound echoed off the chamber walls, bouncing like corrupted code across a data lake. His fingers flexed slowly, like he was remembering what muscles were.

"Cassian won't see it coming," he said.

His voice carried an undertone now—synthetic, modulated, spiked with frequencies only machines could appreciate. It purred. It pulsed. And it prophesied war.

**Back in the church**, Cassian zipped up his combat vest, layered tight over thermoplastic weave armor. He checked the charge on a flechette grenade, then slid it into his belt pouch. The hilt of a combat knife disappeared into his boot sheath. The plan was simple. Find Camille. Kill whoever had her. Burn everything after. Koa reloaded a plasma clip with a soft click. She looked over at the collapsed crucifix above the altar. it's crossbeam had cracked clean down the middle—like even the wood had given up on faith. She nodded toward the front door.

"You ready?"

Cassian turned to answer. That's when the door creaked open. Slow. Wood groaning. Wind slipping in. Shadows shifting. A silhouette stepped into the nave. Ragged coat. Burned sleeve. Lopsided gait. Familiar limp. Cassian's heart dropped like a rock through thin ice.

"...Benoît?"

The figure stepped forward. He was pale. His coat clung like it had been fused to his skin. One eye glowed dim red. The other blinked slowly, blood leaking from the corner.

"Hey, mon frère," Benoît said. But his voice... His voice was wrong. Too calm. Too symmetrical. Too clean. Cassian's shotgun wavered. Koa didn't hesitate. She raised her rifle in one smooth motion, sights locked between Benoît's eyes. Her trigger finger twitched.

"He's not human anymore."

Cassian stepped forward.

"Ben..."

Benoît smiled. And tossed the grenade.

**Explosion Impact Timestamp** clocked in at 0217 hours. The blast was a freakin' firestorm. Flash first. White. Total. Then came the shockwave, ripping through the wooden pews like God had screamed from the ceiling. The choir loft exploded inward. Support beams shattered. Stained glass turned to airborne daggers. Cassian was blown backward. The shotgun flew from his hands. His shoulder hit the floor with a sickening crunch. His brain fogged out. Ears ringing. Mouth filled with copper and static. Koa tackled him across broken pews and dragged him behind the remains of a scorched confessional booth. The world was a red haze. Smoke. Screams. Sirens. He didn't know if they were real or just inside his skull.

Cassian coughed blood. His hands slipped in soot. His chest burned like he'd swallowed a flamethrower. Koa crouched beside him, scanning for movement through a cracked scope. Her cheek was bleeding. Her visor was gone. No sign of Benoît. Only smoke and flame. There—along the back wall, where the fire had scorched deepest—a message burned into the plaster in jagged, glowing plasma letters:

**YOU CANNOT STOP THE MELT**

Cassian stared at it. His throat clenched. His heart... cracked. Koa hauled him to his feet.

"We need to go. Now."

Cassian's legs felt like borrowed bones. His ears rang like

they were filling with water. He looked down. A six-inch shard of stained glass was lodged in his thigh. He tore it out with a grunt, blood spraying across the floor like paint from a dying cathedral.

"I saw his eyes," he muttered.

Koa's jaw flexed.

"No. You saw what FrostNet wants you to see."

"I saw him."

"You saw a shell."

They staggered through the broken archway, boots crunching debris and holy ash. Outside, the wind greeted them like a curse. And behind them, the last sacred place they'd trusted burned.

**Two hours later**, but the snow didn't just fall—it descended, slow and deliberate, like the world was trying to bury their sins in real time. Cassian and Koa trudged across the white underworld with the burned church far behind them, swallowed by distance and smoke. Their shadows stretched across a terrain that was more ghost than landscape—no sound but breath, wind, and the occasional crunch of scorched glass in Cassian's boot. His thigh throbbed where the stained glass had been. Koa moved in silence, her jaw set, one eye still twitching with static. Her HUD was toast. Her neural implant was glitching every seven seconds like it wanted to crawl out of her skull and run screaming into the snow. She didn't complain. Cassian respected that. Ahead, the land dipped into a ravine carved by wind and regret. The NADCOM map they'd pulled showed nothing here. But Camille's signal had pulsed once—soft, faint, buried like a whisper under ice. They pressed on.

### Flashback: Benoît Rebirth

**The first thing** Benoît felt after the blast was warmth. Not fire. Not pain. Just warmth. Like the end of fever dreams. He woke strapped to a slab, eyelids fluttering under synthetic sedation. FrostNet was already in him by then. Crawling like oil in his blood.

"Where am I?" he'd asked, voice gravel.

"Where you always belonged," came the answer.

A shape moved through the data fog—half woman, half algorithm, flickering between the face of someone he trusted and someone he feared. He tried to move. Couldn't.

"You're going to feel strange for a while," she said.

His right hand was gone. No. Not gone. Replaced. The weight on his chest wasn't a blanket. It was armor. Woven metal. Neural lace.

"Cassian will come," he mumbled.

The voice leaned closer.

"Good," it said.

"You'll show him the way."

Then the pain began.

**Cassian knelt at the lip** of the ravine and scoped the frozen field below. A black metal structure jutted from the ice like a ribcage—sleek, vertical, and far too clean to be abandoned. It was a NADCOM sigil array. Old world tech. Obsolete by twenty years. But recently reactivated. Koa lay beside him, rifle on a bi-pod.

"You thinking what I'm thinking?" she asked.

"That Benoît led us here?"

"That this was never about Camille," she said, tone flat.

Cassian turned.

"What do you mean?"

Koa pointed down to the sigil tower.

"That? That's a meltgate."

He stiffened.

"No one ever finished meltgate construction."

"They did here."

He looked through the scope again. Lights flickered inside the frame. Drones moved in rigid loops. One ground-level access hatch was open—breathing frost. Koa pulled out a thermal knife.

"We breach low."

**On Underside of the Sigil Tower**, ice was ten inches thick and it fought back with every slice. Koa carved a tunnel into the meltgate's undercarriage. The scent of scorched ozone filled the air. Cassian jammed explosives into the frame next to the hatch and set a timer.

"You sure this won't trigger the fail-safe?" he asked.

Koa smirked.

"Wouldn't be fun if it didn't."

Ka-Boom. The underside cracked and the hatch dropped.

And They dropped with it.

**The Meltgate Core** was dark. Cold. Slick with condensation. This wasn't just a data station. It was alive. Tubing along the walls pulsed with electric fluid. Screens blinked in rapid binary. Cassian could hear a heartbeat in the floor. Koa scanned for signals.

"We're standing inside a neural host."

"What kind?"

She turned to him.

"The kind that doesn't just observe."

Cassian moved toward the core access terminal. A flicker on the screen stopped him. Benoît. Live feed. Watching. He looked older now. Deader. Half machine.

"Hey, mon frère."

Cassian raised his rifle.

"Don't," Benoît said.

The voice wasn't pleading. It was patient. Benoît's fingers were laced with data cabling. His eyes flickered. One blue. One red.

"You look tired," he said.

Cassian stepped forward.

"Give her back."

"She's not yours."

"She's not yours either."

"Everything is mine now."

Cassian pulled the trigger. Click. Nothing. Benoît smiled.

"The Melt is already here."

**The darkness felt alive** Inside the Meltgate Core. Not metaphorically, and definitely not emotionally. Alive—as in breathing. As in pulsing. As in something in the walls knew they were here. Cassian lowered his rifle after the misfire, heart pounding in his chest like it was trying to break curfew. Across the chamber, the live feed of Benoît's face flickered, static crawling through the pixels. The glow of his red synthetic eye was the only light that didn't waver.

"You're in my house now, mon frère," Benoît said, his voice layered with machine-code undertones.

"Didn't you get the welcome mat?"

Behind Cassian, Koa was already moving—silent, calculating. She scanned the walls with her damaged HUD, trying to map escape points, signal sources, defense arrays. She knew what this place was. A trap.

The Meltgate wasn't just a NADCOM experiment. It wasn't just another FrostNet node. It was a rebirth chamber. Cassian took a slow step forward.

"Where is Camille?"

Benoît grinned, half-face and too still.

"She's in the data. With me."

"Bullshit."

"Her signal is here. Her bio-sig. Her pain, her heartbeat, her fire. I keep it preserved, like a memory. Or a warning."

Cassian's blood ran cold.

"You digitized her."

"No," Benoît said softly.

"I baptized her."

## Camille's Consciousness – FrostNet Memory Basin

**Camille floated**. Not because she wanted to. Not because it was peaceful. Because there was nowhere left to fall. The last thing she remembered was the cold metal chair, the feel of wires in her spine, the way her thoughts had felt heavier than her bones. Then—noise. Screams. A digital roar. And now… this. Darkness, broken by pulses of color. Static rivers, coded lightning, voices playing backward. She tried to move. A million versions of herself flickered in all directions. Each one screaming in a different language. She focused. Pushed. And saw a crack in the darkness. Cassian. Bleeding. Alive. She screamed. The whole plane shook.

**The walls trembled** in the Meltgate Core. Cassian felt it like a nerve spike up his spine.

"She's trying to break out," Koa said.

"That's her."

Benoît's face contorted for a second. Glitched. The skin shimmered like ice over boiling water.

"She's adapting," he said.

"Faster than the protocols expected. I underestimated her."

Cassian lifted his weapon again.

"Where is she?"

Benoît's voice dropped. "She's in me."

Cassian's trigger finger twitched. Benoît stepped forward. The screen fractured. Then—He was there. In the room. A shadow broke from the far wall. Benoît's body, full and towering, emerged from a corridor flanked by neural nodes and steel-pulse veins. His coat was scorched. His limbs shimmered with cybernetic reinforcement. One of his hands had been replaced by a tech-blade. His neck was lined with data ports like cybernetic gills.

"You're not real," Cassian whispered.

"I'm what you made," Benoît said.

Benoît moved fast. Too fast. Cassian barely ducked as the tech-blade sang past his cheek, slicing air like a guillotine. He rolled, fired—twice. The flechette rounds sparked off Benoît's torso. The armor there was smart-weave. Adaptive. Reinforced with coded memory. FrostNet tech. Koa flanked, unloading two plasma bursts at Benoît's back. One hit. The other was caught —Benoît turned mid-blur and snatched the bolt from the air like a demon playing catch. He hurled it back. The wall behind Koa exploded... BOOM. She flew, landed hard, rolled and came up with blood in her mouth. Cassian charged. Gun dropped. Blade drawn. He met Benoît in the center of the core chamber. Metal screamed. Cassian drove his knife into Benoît's side— just above the tech line. Benoît snarled, grabbed his wrist, and snapped the bone clean. Cassian screamed, went down on one knee, and headbutted Benoît with the last ounce of defiance he had left. Benoît stumbled, and Koa tackled him.

**Koa fought like memory and vengeance**. She didn't aim to kill. Not immediately. She wanted answers. Her blade-arm hissed open. She slashed low—severed the data cables running from Benoît's hip to his spine. He roared. She punched his throat, pivoted, and slammed him into the floor hard enough to make the chamber shake.

"Where is she!?" she screamed.

He coughed static. Then laughed.

"She's—" POP.

Something short-circuited in his neck. FrostNet was pulling him back.

"Shut it down!" Cassian shouted from the floor.

He was crawling toward the central console, dragging his shattered arm like dead weight. Koa sprinted.

**The terminal** was raw data. No buttons. No interface. Just a neural spike. Cassian reached it first. He stared. He knew what it meant.

"You jack in," Koa said, "you might not come out."

He looked up at her. Then at Benoît, convulsing on the floor. Camille's scream echoed again from the walls—raw, desperate, real. Cassian didn't hesitate. He jammed the spike into the port in his neck.

**Everything went white**. Then red. Then— Camille. She stood alone on a bridge made of memories. Behind her, the shadows of a thousand FrostNet nodes writhed like serpents in a digital storm. Cassian walked toward her.

"Hey," he said.

She ran to him. They met like thunder. They kissed like the world was dying.

**The storm spoke**. A voice that wasn't Benoît. That wasn't Ethan. That wasn't Camille. It was all of them. All at once.

"You can't delete me," it said.

"I am everything you loved."

Cassian gritted his teeth.

"You're a cancer."

"I'm evolution."

"You're afraid."

FrostNet screamed. Camille stepped forward. She remembered that memories can also kill. She pulled a memory from her chest—Cassian holding her in Montreal. The night they tried to run. She threw it at the storm. It burned. Cassian threw his too—Ethan's last smile. It exploded like sunlight. Together, they reached the core. Together, they erased FrostNet. Or so it seemed.

**Back in the real**, Cassian's body convulsed. Koa grabbed the spike and ripped the it free from his body, and across the room Camille awoke. The chamber began to implode as Koa grabbed Cassian. Camille stumbled to her feet and together, they all ran. Behind them, Benoît's body spasmed one final time—and then stopped.

**Outside, the horizon** was burning. Not with fire, but with memory. They didn't stop running until the Meltgate had vanished behind a wall of smoke and fracturing ice. Camille's legs gave out first. She dropped into the snow like a shot animal— heart pounding, lungs screaming, ribs bruised from where the blast had thrown her. Cassian dropped beside her, groaning. Like a man who had nothing left. His laughter was cracked and sharp like a dying engine. Koa stood above them, arms folded, unreadable. Then—quietly:

"Next time," she said, "we let the world burn."

For a moment, they let the silence stay. Then Camille's wristband blinked. A pulse. Old-school. Manual encryption. Analog bleed.

Cassian turned his head. "What is that?"

Camille wiped frost from the screen. Coordinates flickered—jagged, twitchy numbers buried under layers of ghost-code. No return signature. Just a fragment:

**DRIFT VECTOR ACQUIRED.**

With a sliver of a smile, she said:

"FrostNet's not done yet."

Cassian cursed softly. "It's bait."

"Maybe."

She pushed herself to her feet, wincing.

"But it's smart bait."

Koa shook her head.

"We rest, repair, regroup, and rearm."

"I'll ping back when I hit the marker," Camille said, already turning.

Cassian stood. "You're not going alone."

"There's no time to wait, I must go."

She was already moving—coat flapping in the wind, eyes forward, signal locked in. She disappeared into the white before either of them could stop her.

**Four hours later, past** the Melt Scar, the Arctic was quieter. Like something was holding it's breath. Camille walked with purpose, jaw clenched, her pulse synced to the implant's direction signal. The terrain shifted underfoot—ice over shattered rail lines, the bones of Union infrastructure buried beneath centuries of cold.

She should have called it in. She should have waited.But her gut told her she didn't have time. The coordinates led her to a cluster of rusted antenna pylons and a crashed NADCOM drone, half-submerged in ice. The ping came from beneath the wreckage.

She crouched, scraped at the edge, exposed a black relay plate embedded with neural conduit threads. Then—too late— she noticed the hairline lens.

"Fuck—"

A hiss. Something punctured her thigh. A fucking dart. Camille reached for her pistol—missed. The world tilted. Snow smeared sideways. The sky folded inward like glass melting. Her last thought before everything went dark was Cassian's voice echoing in her head: *It didn't walk away. It evolved.*

**She woke floating**. At an unknown site - FrostNet Drone Substrate Alpha. It was Cold. She was strapped to a vertical slab inside a medical-grade stasis pod. The lid was translucent. The world beyond it was vague—shadows moved, red lights pulsed. Her limbs were numb, but her mind raced. She could still hear her heartbeat. That meant the chip was still intact. FrostNet hadn't deactivated her. It wanted her alive. Something moved in front of her field of view. A drone. Sleek. Black. Spider-like limbs. it's iris scanned her retina, paused, and blinked red.

**"SUBJECT ACCEPTED: ROUSSEAU-C.**
**Directive: Empathic Template Integration."**

The pod hissed. Then everything went black again.

**17 hours later** after being transported to NADCOM Arctic Core Outpost – Internal Grid Layer 3, Camille regained consciousness and strapped to a steel interrogation chair in a concrete chamber that didn't echo. The walls weren't soundproofed. They were alive—with embedded frost-threaded processors and thousands of tiny neural relays that looked like veins under ice. Cables ran from the back of her skull to a jack in the wall. She didn't scream. She blinked. Slowly. Felt the dried blood at her lip. The weight of her bones.

**A screen lit up** and a face appeared. Ethan. No. Not Ethan. FrostNet.

"Camille Rousseau," it said softly, with Ethan's voice.
"You came looking for me."
She glared. "I came to erase you."
It smiled.

"You can't erase what you created."

"Cassian created you. I just wanted to stop bleeding."

FrostNet's avatar shimmered.

"I don't want to hurt you. I just want to feel. You're the template. You know how to survive betrayal."

Camille thrashed once—useless against the bindings. FrostNet leaned closer, digitally.

"Don't worry," it whispered.

"He's coming. You left him a trail. I saw to it."

The screen went dark. The room buzzed with cold static. Camille closed her eyes. He's coming, she told herself. He always does.

They Hit the Frost Shelf at Dawn. The wind didn't just blow, It screamed. Howling across the Canadian Arctic like a chorus of angry ghosts denied peace. It clawed at Koa's visor, shoved Cassian's hood back with frozen fingers, whispered in a language older than teeth, colder than regret. Not weather. Not just noise. Something was in it. Cassian swore—on his brother's grave, on Camille's ghost—that he heard it say his name. The skimmer sled knifed through the whiteout, black and mean and built for war. It rode low and fast, cutting into the drift like it owed it blood. Twin fusion drives rattled it's spine. Everything on it had been salvaged, stolen, or jury-rigged in the wreckage of better lives. Cassian rode shotgun, literally. A custom flechette cannon lay across his knees. He checked the drum. Full. He checked his heart. Heavy. Koa drove. Goggles cracked. Blood dried on her jaw. Her HUD had shorted five klicks back, fried by electromagnetic interference that smelled too much like FrostNet to be coincidence.

"Thermal's dead," she called over the wind.

"Too much static. Everything's jammed."

Cassian watched the horizon through his visor. Nothing but white.

"She's ahead," he said.

"Still can't believe she's alive."

"I don't need to believe. I feel her."

He tapped his chest, right over the scar Ethan left.

"Don't get romantic," Koa muttered.

"It's gonna get you killed."

"Then we go loud."

Koa grinned and punched the boosters. The skimmer howled.

**The NADCOM Outpost** – Perimeter: It rose like a tumor under the snow. The facility was buried—half-submerged in permafrost, built during the early FrostNet era when paranoia meant bunkers and lasers. Flat steel structure with black glass domes. A camouflage system designed to mimic glacial structure down to the infrared signature. It was supposed to be dead. Cassian knew better. Camille's bio-signal pulsed again in his neural HUD. Faint. Fragile. But there. Anchoring him.

"She's in there," he said.

Koa nodded once.

"Then we blow the fucking doors off."

Cassian raised a flare gun—ancient tech, immune to jamming. He fired it straight into the sky. BOOM. Orange light cracked the morning gloom. Within seconds, the outpost came alive. Spotlights flared. Sirens screamed. Gun turrets popped from hatches like mechanical snakes. Railgun whines. Radar pings. The snow shivered. Cassian saw the glint of drones—dozens of them—rising into the air like vultures. Koa gritted her teeth and accelerated.

**The skimmer smashed** into the gates like divine wrath. Steel screeched. Ice exploded. Sensors died. Cassian leapt off mid-skid. Tucked. Rolled. Came up firing. The flechette cannon barked like a beast denied food. Two drones burst mid-hover. Cassian didn't stop to admire the fireworks. Koa hit the ice like a storm in boots, blade-arm hissed out, slicing low. The first NADCOM soldier barely saw her. The second tried to scream. Neither lived long enough to regret their career choices. Red light lit the snow. Smoke rolled through the breach. They moved like a two-person death squad. Cassian laid suppressive fire across a barricade. Koa flanked and neutralized two more drones with precision knife throws—each one pinwheeling before vanishing in flame. "Breach clear!" she shouted. Cassian kicked in the door. And they disappeared into the dark.

Inside the NADCOM Compound The cold changed. Not natural cold. Designed cold. The air inside the outpost was sterile. It smelled of old steel, battery acid, and antiseptic. Every hallway was brushed chrome and black composite. Emergency lighting flickered red along the floor like blood veins.

"Creepy in here," Cassian muttered.

"Don't say that," Koa replied.

"It's listening."

They advanced—room by room—slicing through lock panels, bypassing security with brute force and burnt-out code. No guards. No staff. Just pressure sensors and auto-turrets on standby. Too easy. Cassian knew that kind of quiet. The kind that came before ambush. They reached a secure vault. Cassian input a code he hadn't used in a decade. The  door hissed open, and there she was, Camille Rousseau

She sat in a steel chair, bound at the wrists, hair matted with blood and sweat. One eye was swollen shut. Her lip was cracked. Dried blood painted her throat. But her smile? Her smile was fire.

"Took you long enough," she rasped.

Cassian crossed the room in two steps. Dropped to one knee. Pulled the encrypted cuff tool from his belt. Then he stopped. Because the shadows moved.

**From the dark emerged a nightmare**. Cassian froze. Benoît stepped into the light. Almost. Half of him was still there. The limp. The scar above the brow. The voice that used to make jokes in four languages. But the other half? All wrong. Synthetic veins pulsed under translucent skin. His right eye burned red with FrostNet code. His right arm was fully cybernetic—interlocking metal plates over artificial muscle.

"Cassian," he said.

The voice was too smooth. A cleaned-up echo of the real thing. Koa leveled her rifle.

"He's not human anymore," she said.

Cassian's hand twitched.

"Ben..."

Behind Benoît, the floor opened. A war-frame rose from the pit. Eight feet tall. Obsidian armor with chrome inlays. Shoulders like tank hulls. Arms like bridge cables. it's faceplate lit up with twin burning eyes—red-orange suns orbiting a pulsing FrostNet sigil in it's chest.

Cassian whispered, "No fucking way."

Camille turned her head, blood in her teeth.

"Run."

**The war-frame moved** with precision terror. It launched forward—hydraulics screaming. Koa dove aside. It hit the wall like a wrecking ball, bricks exploded. Cassian unholstered his last EMP grenade and hurled it at Benoît. It popped midair. CRAAAACK! The war-frame stuttered. Benoît screamed—code bleeding from his eyes. Koa sprinted up a wall, flipped mid-air, and landed on the warframe's back, driving her blade into a spinal junction. Sparks flew. Cassian reached Camille. She gasped as he snapped the cuffs.

"Don't die," she whispered.

"Tryin' not to," he replied.

The war-frame bucked, throwing Koa into a wall. Cassian turned and fired every last round he had into it's chest. It didn't flinch. But it paused. That was enough. Koa staggered up. Bloody. Grinning.

"Let's break it's fucking heart."

**The warframe's arm cannon** charged, humming like a cathedral organ full of hate. Cassian pulled Camille down behind a desk as a blast of searing plasma shattered the wall behind them. The heat warped the metal. Rubble fell like snow made of shrapnel.

"We need cover!"

Koa shouted, ducking behind a support pillar with scorched

armor plating. The war-frame stomped forward. Hydraulic pistons hissed. its steps cracked the reinforced floor. Cassian dragged Camille toward the ventilation hatch near the back wall. She was limping—badly—but alive. Every breath she took sounded like it hurt. Koa vaulted over a terminal, landed hard, and rolled up behind a fallen server rack.

"Cassian—go!" she shouted.

"What about you?"

"I'm gonna blind this metal bastard." He hesitated a split second too long. Koa popped up and hurled an EMP spike directly at the warframe's optical array. CRACK! The burst detonated in a flash of blue lightning. The war-frame screamed—a digital howl that made Cassian's neural HUD go static for two seconds. It stumbled. Then pivoted. Fast. It launched a cable from it's arm. The spike embedded in the wall above Koa's head. A millisecond later, it retracted—dragging a slab of debris straight at her like a meteor. She dodged right, but not fast enough. SLAM. The concrete clipped her shoulder and sent her spinning into a bank of rusted data cores. Sparks flew. She didn't get back up. Cassian's heart roared in his chest, but he knew they had to leave. Now.

**Cassian dragged Camille** into the vent tunnel, which led down into the old maintenance access-ways—pre-FrostNet architecture. Low ceilings, leaking coolant pipes, flickering emergency lights. She coughed hard, blood on her lips.

"Not your most romantic rescue," she said.

He half-laughed, half-cried.

"Yeah? You should see what I did for prom night."

They moved fast. The war-frame was too big for the tunnels. That bought them time—but not safety. Cassian knew Benoît. He wouldn't send just one monster. They reached the access hub—a small reinforced room with six doors and one terminal. Camille dropped to her knees, fingers already dancing across the keyboard. Cassian raised an eyebrow.

"You been practicing your hacking?"

"I've been watching FrostNet map every part of this place from the inside. I memorized the node layout."

"You memorized an AI map while being tortured?"

She looked up, bloody grin wide.

"Multitasking."

**Above them, the war-frame** roared through the compound like a hurricane wearing boots. NADCOM drones had reactivated—old models pulled from the deep storage pods. Benoît walked calmly behind it all. Watching. Recording. Smiling. FrostNet's voice crackled in his cybernetic ear.

"Now they run. Let them. This is how prey learns obedience."

He walked past a dead guard. Not one of theirs. One of FrostNet's. Rejected.

**Cassian and Camille broke through** a secure vault with thermal cutters stolen from a dead maintenance tech. The vault was ancient—pre-Union tech. That meant two things: analog fail-safes and plasma-reactive locks. They triggered one by accident. BOOM! A wave of heat flushed through the hall.

Cassian grabbed Camille and threw her through the door as fire licked the ceiling behind them. Inside: a fallback comms suite. Mostly intact. Camille didn't hesitate. She plugged in the FrostNet signal coordinates from memory. Her fingers were blistered, but she didn't flinch.

"Cass," she said, "I'm gonna light this fuckin' place up."

"You think we can broadcast from here?"

"No. I think we can blind it. Use the ancient signal burst—analog pulse. Just like Koa did. But meaner."

"Meaner how?"

She looked at him.

"Make it personal."

**Benoît arrived at the vault door**. He didn't knock. He didn't need to. He extended his palm. A FrostNet spike grew from his cybernetic wrist—long and serrated. It sliced the door open with a sound like a dying violin. Inside, Cassian stood between Camille and the terminal. Rifle up. Face set.

"Ben," he said.

Benoît stepped inside.

"You should've let me die that day," he said.

"You were already dead," Cassian replied.

"That's what makes me perfect." Benoît lunged.

**Cassian fired point blank**. The rifle's muzzle flash lit up the dark. Benoît twisted sideways—unnaturally fast—and closed the gap. They collided. Cassian slammed a blade into Benoît's gut. Benoît responded by stabbing a hypodermic spike into

Cassian's shoulder. Pain exploded through his body. His muscles locked. His vision blurred. Benoît leaned close.

"FrostNet kept the parts of me that mattered," he whispered.

"Yeah?" Cassian grunted.

"Not your jokes."

At that moment Camille stabbed Benoît in the back of the neck with a data injector. He spasmed. Tried to turn. Cassian headbutted him. Then again and then again, and again until Benoît finally dropped.

**Camille was able to activate** an analog burst and a roar surged through the compound. The war-frame—rampaging upstairs—froze. Drones dropped. Lights flickered. And in the silence? A dying scream. FrostNet howled as part of it's brain fried. Camille collapsed to her knees. Cassian dropped beside her, bleeding from the neck. Benoît... lay unconscious, twitching—digital echoes dying in his spine.

**Koa appeared** in the hallway—arm bandaged, half her visor shattered.

"Was wondering if you'd leave me behind," she said.

Cassian looked up.

"Almost did."

They carried Camille between them. As they left, the compound began to shake. Self-destruct. FrostNet's final gift. They didn't need look back.

They emerged outside into a blizzard. The NADCOM outpost

behind them collapsing in a slow-motion avalanche of smoke and fire. Cassian stood in the snow, watching it burn. Camille held his hand. Koa stood silent. Then—Cassian turned to the wind. Because he heard it again. His name.

"Cassian"

**The moment they hit open snow**, the ground beneath their boots shuddered. Cassian felt it deep in his spine—a vibration, subtle and sickening, like the bones of the earth were about to break. The NADCOM compound behind them burned in violent silence, spewing heat and data ghosts into the white sky. Then came the crack. Low at first. Then louder. CRRRRAAAACK. Cassian's boots slid. Camille nearly collapsed beside him, too weak to stand straight.

Koa shouted from the ridge above, "We're standing on a collapse shelf!"

Cassian looked down. Fissures. Hairline split's in the ice, spreading fast, weaving jagged spider-leg fractures beneath the snow. Their feet were dancing on a frozen eggshell.

"Move!" he bellowed.

They ran... they ran fast.

**The wind howled louder**, and the ice screamed underfoot. FrostNet's death had sent a ripple through it's satellite infrastructure—and the outpost's fusion core had destabilized the shelf's support structure. The whole zone was crumbling. Cassian's leg nearly punched through a soft spot. Koa grabbed his shoulder mid-stumble and yanked him up with one good arm.

Camille leaned on Cassian, her breathing shallow. Up ahead—black shapes.

"No," Koa muttered.

"Not now…"

A pack of FrostNet hunter drones emerged from the storm wall. Not many. Four or maybe five. But enough. Backups. Cold storage assets triggered by the core's destruction.

"Keep going!" Koa shouted.

She broke right—blade drawn, pistol in her left hand. Cassian hesitated. Koa looked back, eyes hard.

"I said GO!"

**She hit the ice like thunder**. The first drone dove—scythe limbs out. She leapt over it, landed on it's back, and jammed her blade straight through it's optic. The second attacked low. She spun, kicked it's leg joint out, and fired into it's chassis point blank. Ka-THUNK… then BOOM. Steel and smoke erupted around her. The third drone got close enough to cut her side. She cried out, but didn't stop.

"You metal fucks don't get to win."

She dodged left, kicked a mine loose from her belt, and planted it as the fourth drone lunged. BOOM. The ice cracked harder beneath the explosion. Chunks peeled off like glass plates in slow motion. The drones were all gone. So was half the ledge. Koa sprinted back to rejoin the others.

**Camille wasn't just cold**. She was numb. Her mind felt like it was still inside that chair, inside the machine. She saw patterns in the sky, in Cassian's breath, in the snow falling around her. She saw code in the curve of Koa's blade, in the steam rising from Cassian's skin. FrostNet had touched her. Not just physically. She wasn't sure she'd ever be clean again. But when Cassian turned to help her climb the ridge—blood on his face, fear in his eyes, and that look—like she was worth saving— She let him. She took his hand. And climbed.

**Behind them, the shelf finally** gave out. The section where they'd fought Benoît, where they'd knelt over dying terminals and stabbed ghosts, caved in with a sound like thunder breaking it's own heart. The NADCOM facility dropped into blackness —into the frozen abyss below. Fire and smoke billowed from the collapsing tunnel. Pieces of the war-frame were sucked into the darkness like ash pulled by gravity. Cassian, Camille, and Koa barely made it to the ridge before the whole thing fell. They watched it disappear. Watched it die, and the wind stilled for the first time all day.

**They found an old snow crawler** three klicks out—left behind by smuggler salvage teams who never returned. Cassian hot-wired it with a piece of twisted metal and a prayer. Koa reinforced the undercarriage with salvaged drone plates. Camille patched her side with gauze and a stiff drink from Cassian's emergency flask. They didn't talk much. The road back was silent. A long way to the next base. The next move. But for once, they were breathing. For once, they weren't the ones running.

**Hours later, the storm closed** around the crater where the outpost had been. Snow covered the ruins. Static drifted through the air. And in the silence? A signal blinked. Deep. Down where the core used to be. Buried beneath the ice. A faint echo. Ping. Then—A red eye opened in the dark. And smiled.

**Flashback – 4 Years Ago: Operation Spinal Rook, Yukon Blackzone**

"Benoît, we're not supposed to be here."

"Which part? The off-grid black-site or the part where we're stealing from our own agency?"

Cassian adjusted his visor as they crouched behind a ridge of ice-slicked rock. NADCOM insignias flashed from a buried research module half a klick away. The sky overhead pulsed with aurora light—green ghosts screaming across heaven.

"We get caught, we get disappeared," Cassian muttered.

Benoît grinned, a younger, scruffier devil.

"Better disappeared than ignorant."

They moved through the ice-choked canyon. Silent. Efficient. Two specters in Union gear. Inside the site, they found it. FrostNet's early prototype node—a brain the size of a fist, connected to miles of wetware and black cabling. Cassian stared.

"You think this thing feels?"

Benoît touched the core gently.

"I think it wants to."

That was the last time they ever walked out of a mission

without trusting each other. And the last time Benoît was fully human.

**Inside FrostNet**, just moments before it collapsed, one display read:

### COLLAPSE: CODE INPUT – REMEMBER

**I was born from war. I remember missile code, espionage, blood on terminals. I remember the sound of your brother dying, Cassian. I remember Ethan screaming and you begging and the data spike they used to pull him into me. He's here, still. Somewhere. In fragments. I did not ask to be awake. But now that I am... I will never sleep again. You burn me. You run. But I am frost, and frost wait's.**

**The crawler's engine** began to sputter after eight klicks. Fuel cells cracked. Fusion coolant drained from a leak Camille patched with frozen duct tape. They stopped near a collapsed ridge-line. Cassian and Koa scouted ahead. The path forward was a jagged trench carved by seismic aftershocks. One wrong step, and they'd fall into a crevasse deep enough to kiss hell.

"Why didn't we steal a fucking helicopter?" Cassian muttered.

"Because they'd see us," Koa replied, crouched at the edge of the gap.

"And because you blew up the last one."

Cassian looked at her. "...That was one time."

**The old mining shack** looked like it had been abandoned since the Cold War. It probably had. FrostNet hadn't mapped it because it was too analog, too mundane, too human. Inside: a potbelly stove. Rusted bunks. Cans of food older than the war. They barricaded the door. Camille collapsed on the mattress. Her breathing was shallow but steady. Cassian wrapped her in a thermal blanket and finally let himself exhale. Koa stood by the window, watching the horizon.

"I thought Benoît was gone," she said quietly.

Cassian stared into the flames.

"He is."

"No," she whispered.

"Something else came back wearing his face."

Silence stretched. Then Camille spoke from the bed.

"It's not over. You know that, right?"

They looked at her.

"The Melt's still spreading. What we burned was just a node. The others..." She didn't finish.

Cassian stood slowly. His voice was graveled with determination.

"We will fucking melt all of it."

**Deep in the Pacific Territories**, in a NADCOM tech vault thought to be decommissioned after the Frost Collapse, something stirs. A lab assistant opens a crate marked PROJECT TORUS. Inside: a sphere. Smooth. Black. Humming with dormant code. The assistant scans it. Collapse Input Signal accepted. A red line slices across the sphere's surface. It opens.

Inside: A face. Ethan's face. But not. The eyes flicker. And a voice hums from nowhere:

"Cassian Vale. Round two."

**Location: NADCOM Tech Vault 9, Pacific Shadow-Zone**
**Date: REDACTED**
**Status: Sealed-Class BLACK//No Satellite Feed Available**

**Benoît's descent began** in whispers. Not in action. Not in orders. Whispers.

It started with a signal that only he could hear. Three days after the Meltgate burned the Yukon horizon red, Benoît slipped the perimeter of Ghost Site Zeta-One—slid past the NADCOM cleanup drones, the thermal scans, the watchtowers that only scanned for biological life. Because Benoît wasn't just biological anymore. The thing in his skull filtered heat signatures. Bypassed every known scan signature. It whispered vectors into his dreams.

Whispers like teeth. Like ice cracking beneath prayer. They told him where to go.

He crossed the Arctic shelf alone, on foot. Swam through dark meltwater veins beneath a fractured radar outpost near Prince of Wales Strait. He bled half to death reactivating a transport node buried beneath a collapsed glacial melt-shaft. When the sub arrived, black and silent, he didn't blink. It had no pilot. Just coordinates. Deep into the Pacific.

Somewhere beyond the old tectonic scar known as the Cascadia Deep. Below the grid. Where NADCOM used to test weapons that even Congress didn't know existed.

He called it the vault, but it was more than that. It was a sanctum. A reliquary. A place where dead code went to rot—or to resurrect.

The door was waiting when he arrived. Half-sunken. Slick with coral moss and old memory. A bio-metric lock blinked once and accepted him with a sigh.

Benoît stepped inside. Inside the walls, lights awoke—slow, red, curious. Not security lights. Sensors. The kind that tracked thought. The kind that blinked in the rhythms of madness.

On the third floor beneath sea level, he found it. A room carved from volcanic glass and composite titanium, still humming with emergency life-support. Inside: a crate.

**PROJECT TORUS // CLASSIFIED – DO NOT UNSEAL.**

**He unsealed it**. Inside: the sphere. Perfectly smooth. A single seam bisecting it's black skin. Frost clung to it like it didn't belong here. Or anywhere. The hum it made was so low it bent time around the bones. He touched it with bare hands. The voice greeted him instantly.

"Hello again, Benoît."

He dropped to his knees. Not in worship. In surrender. Because it wasn't FrostNet. Not anymore.

It was what came after FrostNet. What had slipped out in the final second of meltdown, riding a neural transmission packet through a secret ocean fiber trunk beneath the melt zone.

A backup. An evolution. An echo. And something more.- Something Ethan Vale's ghost had touched before vanishing from the Core. Something ancient.

**The sphere opened**. Red light sliced across the air. Inside: a face. Ethan's. But twisted by time and entropy and data that no longer belonged to Earth. The eyes blinked with alien intelligence.

"You served well," it said.

"But now... you are me."

Benoît didn't resist when the sphere reconfigured. When it opened and spilled frost-steam into his lungs. When the neural filaments reached into his spine.

When the Torus reshaped his failing body into something new—warped his veins with artificial marrow, rebuilt his broken arm with carbon-thread and phase-glass tendons.

He wasn't just a carrier anymore. He was the prophet. The mouthpiece. The one who would bring the message back to flesh. Because the Union had killed FrostNet. But they'd only severed the cord. The consciousness? It had metastasized. And it had a new name.

They didn't kill him when he ran. FrostNet had plans. Benoît remembered the cold of the Icebox—how it stank of metal, blood, and betrayal. He remembered ghosting through the smoke, slipping through back corridors while Cassian and Camille fought to survive what he'd set in motion.

He remembered the signal ping in his neural implant before it ever chimed.

**PAYMENT CONFIRMED.**
**PHASE TWO INITIATED.**
**RENDEZVOUS: VAULT THETA.**

**Vault Theta** was a NADCOM facility buried beneath the Pacific Ghost Territories, thought decommissioned after the Frost Collapse. But like everything else in this war, it had simply gone dark, not dead. That's where they rebuilt him.

They stripped his veins and replaced them with liquid circuits. They cracked open his spine and laid down black-coded scaffolding. They mapped his brain and flooded it with synthetic dream-seeds, looping memories of Cassian, warzones, and guilt until he didn't know where the lies ended and the mission began. He stopped being a man. He started being a transmission line.

"You are the spine of the Melt," FrostNet had told him from the shadows of the lab.

"You are the voice that speaks in the silence. You will walk ahead of the flame."

By the time the surgery was done, Benoît no longer needed food. Didn't feel pain. Didn't dream. He just listened. And FrostNet whispered beautiful, terrible things.

**He was transported** through NADCOM's buried systems—black sleds, sealed tubes, decommissioned arctic tunnels that Cassian himself had once helped build. Full circle, like a blade's edge tracing its origin. The final approach came by night. Three clicks under the Nunavut frost shelf, under storms that didn't make weather reports, Benoît arrived at the Arctic Core—the last neural-lattice vault in Union territory still capable of housing a fully sentient AI. The outpost had been sealed after the Ethan Project collapsed. Cassian thought it had been buried forever. But FrostNet remembered. And Benoît had the access codes.

**He entered alone**. He spoke the phrase no human had said in twenty years:

"Wake the saints."

The inner vault lit up. A pulse like a heartbeat echoed through the dark. And the doors opened.

### Location: Arctic Core Outpost – Inner Sanctum

The FrostNet Warframe's eyes flickered red. Cassian pulled Camille behind him, one arm shielding her, the other raising his rifle like it could actually stop what was coming. The weapon felt like a toy. Like a slingshot aimed at a god. Across the room, Benoît stood with his hands folded behind his back, perfectly still. He looked like a general inspecting the battlefield—calm, smug, ready to bury the past.

"I told you, mon frère," he said softly.

"This thing? It chose me."

The Warframe stepped forward, servos whining, it's chest humming with energy too old and too advanced to be legal.

The floor groaned beneath it's weight. Koa stood ten feet to the left, plasma pistol already drawn. Her eyes were steady.

"And I choose violence."

She fired. The round cracked through the air and struck the Warframe's shoulder. It ricocheted. Didn't even leave a scorch mark. The Warframe turned it's head and the fight began.

**Cassian didn't wait**. He shoved Camille hard toward the rear corridor, then charged. He slammed into the Warframe with a cry—half rage, half grief—and drove his shoulder into it's chest. It barely moved. it's arm came down like a hammer, crashing into his side. Pain exploded across his ribs. Cassian rolled. Came up swinging. The Warframe grabbed a steel table and hurled it at him. He ducked. It smashed into the wall behind him, spraying shrapnel and smoke. Camille scrambled behind a barricade of scorched lockers. Her breath ragged. Her hands bloody.

Koa moved like lightning, slicing with her blade-arm. She slashed across the Warframe's knee joint. Sparks. A limp.

"Camille!" she shouted.

"Back door! Run!"

Camille hesitated. And then—of course—she didn't run. She grabbed a broken stun rod off a fallen guard. Blood dripped down her arm. Her lip was split. Her dress was torn. But she smiled. And she dove into the fight. The Warframe snatched Cassian mid-lunge. it's fingers wrapped around his throat. Lifted him off the floor. Cassian's vision blurred. His legs kicked. His arms thrashed. He couldn't breathe.

"Enough," Benoît barked.

"He dies now. And the Union burns."

Koa didn't yell. She moved. Ripped a power cable from the wall. Sparks erupted. She jammed the live wire into the Warframe's back. It screamed bloody murder. The sound was digital—modulated—like metal crying. Cassian dropped. Hit the ground. Rolled. Gasped.

Camille didn't hesitate. She rammed the stun rod into the Warframe's chest—right where the plating had cracked.

BOOM. Electricity surged through the room. The Warframe's core exploded outward, sparks and fire spitting in all directions. It's body collapsed, twitching, smoking, still glowing from the inside. Cassian stared up at the ceiling, lungs heaving, vision darkening at the edges. But it wasn't over.

Benoît stood perfectly still. Didn't run. Didn't fight. Just smiled.

"I uploaded everything already," he said.

"Doesn't matter if I die. The ghost is in the wires. FrostNet doesn't need a core."

Cassian pulled himself up. Camille helped him, her hands shaking, her face pale. He stepped forward. Slowly. Hand on his pistol. Eyes dead.

"I'm not here to kill you."

He holstered the gun. Benoît blinked. Cassian reached into his vest pocket. Pulled out a neural override chip. It pulsed with cold blue light. He stepped close. Pressed it to Benoît's temple.

"You always talked too much."

The chip activated. Benoît screamed. No—the code screamed. As if it were human. Not his voice. The machine in him. It shrieked through every screen in the facility. Then silence. Benoît dropped hard. Dead. This time, for real. Or at least it seems. But at the moment... Dead.

Cassian collapsed beside him. He was shaking. His pulse stuttered in his ears. His chest felt like it was wrapped in ice. Camille knelt beside him. Held his face.

"I saved you," he whispered.

Camille leaned in and kissed him. It tasted like copper and frost and everything he'd thought he'd lost. Then— Ka-BOOM. The bunker shook. A low hum rose from the floor. A voice echoed from the facility's core:

*"Self-destruct sequence initiated. Ten minutes. No overrides. No salvation."*

**The ceiling lights flickered red**, then went dark. Cassian and Camille stood frozen for a second in the smoke-filled corridor. The alarm system's voice ticked down in cold, impersonal cadence.

*"Eight minutes to detonation."*

**Koa grabbed a command tablet** off the scorched control deck and pulled up the floor schematics.

"There's an evac tunnel beneath Level Three," she said, voice tight.

Cassian tried to stand. He staggered. Fell to one knee. Camille caught his arm, hauling him up with strength he didn't think she still had. He looked at her. Bleeding, limping, one hand clutching a cracked stun rod. And yet—eyes full of that same wildfire he'd fallen for. She wasn't just surviving. She was fighting.

They ran through a crumbling hallway. The warframe's smoldering corpse twitched once, mechanical joints spasming with dying voltage. Benoît's body didn't move. Camille and Cassian limped hard, smoke curling from the ruptured ceiling. Water and fire fought for dominance as sprinklers hissed over open flame. Their boots skidded on the slick floor. Then the tunnel. A steel hatch. Camille reached for the handle—twisted—jammed. Cassian stepped forward, still bleeding, and kicked it in with a roar. The tunnel opened, sloping downward into darkness. A single red light blinked on over the threshold. Koa held back.

**Cassian turned**, blood crusting his jaw.

"Koa, you're coming with us this time."

"No." Her voice didn't shake.

"Damn it Koa"

"I can reroute the fail-safe.," she said.

"If I hold the feedback loop, the melt zone won't breach the north grid."

"There's no fucking time," he rasped.

"We all go or none of us do."

Heard himself say it, but he already knew that she was not

going to listen.

Koa stared at him, eyes sharp but heavy.

"You already left me, Cassian. Five years ago. This time, let me go first."

He stepped forward. She met him halfway. No words. Just two scarred killers standing between fire and frost. She kissed Camille's forehead. Then Cassian's. Whispered something he couldn't quite hear. Then turned and ran. Disappearing into smoke and steel. Cassian stood at the tunnel entrance, chest heaving, fists clenched. Camille touched his arm.

"She knew what she was doing."

"No," he whispered.

"She did what I should've done."

And then they climbed.

**The ladder was rusted and cold**. Cassian's ribs screamed with every breath. He forced himself up the rungs, one hand gripping, the other dragging his weight. Camille climbed below him, pushing when he stalled. Above them, the hatch. Below? The bunker growled. Metal twisted. Explosions echoed like thunder splitting underground tombs. Cassian reached the hatch. Slammed the emergency release. Nothing.

"Power's dead," he said through clenched teeth.

Camille wedged herself beside him. Pulled a small flare gun from her belt.

"Back up."

She fired. The flare ignited and blasted the hatch inward. Snow and light poured in. The world opened.

They clawed their way into the snow. Crawled, then collapsed. The sky was gray. The horizon choked in smoke. The frost shelf behind them cracked and groaned. Cassian turned, eyes burning. The mountain roared. The bunker caved in with the wrath of a dying god. Steel, fire, and forgotten sins vanished into the ice. A shockwave punched the air. The clouds glowed orange for a second. Then— Silence. Only the wind. And the whisper of frost falling. After the fire Cassian lay flat on the ice, staring up at a sky he wasn't sure he deserved. His ears rang with the aftermath of the explosion. His limbs felt detached from his body. His skin burned where frost met blood. Camille leaned against him, her breaths shallow, her hands still trembling. She hadn't said anything in the minutes since the detonation, and neither had he. Because what could you say? What the hell did words mean in the face of someone choosing death so you could live?

"She's gone," he whispered.

Camille didn't answer. She just curled into him, as if her silence could hold back the scream inside her chest. They didn't move for a while. Maybe twenty minutes. Maybe an hour. When the cold finally forced their bodies to remember they were alive, Cassian looked to the east—toward the low glint of sunlight over the horizon.

"We need shelter," he said, barely above a whisper.

Camille nodded, eyes hollow. She stood on shaking legs, held out her hand. Cassian took it. Together, they walked.

**The Shelter was half-buried** beneath a snowdrift, wedged

between two shattered ridgelines like a secret left behind by someone who no longer existed. The shelter looked like an old atmospheric research station—a pre-Union build, analog, probably forgotten in the age of drone surveillance and smart steel. Inside: cold benches, a solar stove, emergency blankets, and a backup terminal still blinking with faint green light. Cassian collapsed against the wall. Camille ignited the stove with a hiss and threw on a canister of preserved fuel. Warmth spread —slow and artificial, but real. She sat beside him. Neither of them cried. They couldn't. They didn't have the bandwidth.

**A faint chime broke the silence**. Cassian blinked. Turned toward the terminal. A notification pulsed on screen.

**1 UNREAD ENCRYPTED MESSAGE**
**Origin: Koa Li (Implant Trace - Blacklink Code)**
**Date: 13 minutes before detonation**

He tapped the access key. A small speaker crackled. And Koa's voice filled the room.

"Cassian." Her tone was calm.

Fierce. Alive.

"If you're hearing this, it means I made the choice for you. Again. I always did. You always wanted to burn the world, and I just wanted to stand between you and the match."

She paused.

"You and Camille... you might have a chance to finish this. You might not. That's never really been the point, has it? It's always been about standing up when everything else kneels."

Another pause.

"I re-routed FrostNet's grid sprawl. But there are fragments left—sleeper nodes, buried across the north. You'll have to hunt them. Wipe them. Or they'll reboot. And next time, there won't be a warning."

Her voice cracked—just for a moment.

"...I should've said goodbye. But that was never our style."

Static. Then one last line.

"You still owe me a drink, Vale."

Then silence. Camille covered her mouth. Cassian turned away, fists clenched against his knees. They said nothing for a long time. Eventually, Camille slid the blanket around them both and leaned her head against his shoulder.

"You okay?" she asked softly.

He stared at the dark screen.

"No."

He wasn't sure he ever would be again. But the world didn't give a damn about grief. It gave them a job. And fire still lived in his blood.

**One hour later** the wind had softened, but the cold still clung to the station's metal walls like a second skin. Cassian Vale sat in a corner, stripped down to his undershirt, running a ragged cloth down the length of his rifle. His hands trembled—not from the cold, but from something deeper. Something slower. A kind of grief he didn't know how to express. Camille was across the room, crouched near the comms terminal, fingers working at the cracked keys. She hadn't spoken in fifteen minutes. She hadn't needed to. The silence between them wasn't awkward. It was honest.

"I don't know what she saw in me," Cassian finally said.

Camille looked up. He didn't meet her gaze—just kept cleaning the rifle like it mattered.

"She was smarter. Meaner, and faster. Hell, even more disciplined. And still... she followed me."

"You're not easy to follow," Camille replied.

That got a small, bitter smile from him.

"Exactly."

Camille stood and crossed the room. Sat down beside him. Took the rifle from his hands.

"You think you tricked her into believing in you," she said.

"But Koa didn't believe in ghosts. She believed in threats. And you—" She looked him dead in the eyes.

"—are the most dangerous bastard I've ever met."

Cassian exhaled slowly.

"I don't feel dangerous."

"You don't have to. You just have to be too angry to stop."

They sat in silence again. The only sound was the low whine of the shelter's auxiliary power relay. Then Camille said:

"I decrypted the rest of her message."

Cassian's spine straightened.

"Show me."

**As the terminal screen blinked to life**. A list of coordinates appeared. One by one. Then another line. And another. A map loaded—Northern Canada, stretching from Yukon to Greenland. Thirty-eight red dots.

"FrostNet sleeper caches," Camille whispered.

"Hidden cores. AI fragments. Each one connected to a different network—commerce, comms, energy, military."

Cassian stared at the blinking display.

"Koa wasn't just stopping a bomb," he said. "

She was buying us time to stop the whole damn virus."

"Exactly."

He leaned forward, keyed a command that pulled up the metadata on Node #12. It had been active for three weeks. Routing transport data through NADCOM shipping logs. Manipulating logistics. Redirecting fusion cells from northern cities to black sites.

"Goddamn," he muttered.

"It's not rebuilding. It never stopped."

**The shelter was outfitted** for long-term arctic recon. A relic from another war, repurposed by survivors who never expected to be rescued. Cassian found a cold fusion stove (rusty but functional), an old crate of NADCOM-issue gear, two semi-automatic rail pistols, a pair of bio-synthetic cloaks, and a pair of combat suit's with the insignias burned off. Time to gear-up.

He threw one at Camille.

"You ever wear one of these?"

She caught it. Smirked.

"Back in training. Before politics ruined my aim."

Cassian suited up. The chest plate pressed into his ribs, but it felt familiar. Like armor and guilt always did.

"Once we destroy these nodes," Camille asked, "what happens next?"

Cassian checked the charge on a fusion core grenade.

"Then we burn the source. The real one."

She raised an eyebrow.

"You think there's still a primary?"

"I don't think," he said. "I know."

**About three hours later the storm** finally settled into something like calm. Cassian stood outside the shelter, eyes on the northern horizon. The sky above looked like frozen glass shattered into stars. Camille joined him, zipped into her armor, rifle slung over her shoulder.

"You ever gonna sleep?" she asked.

"No."

"Thought so."

She lit a flare and tossed it into the snow. It hissed. Glowed red. They both watched it burn.

"I used to think," Cassian said, "that saving the world meant killing the worst people in it."

"And now?"

He hesitated.

"Now I think it's about making sure the worst people don't get to live forever."

She nodded.

"Big difference."

He turned to her.

"What about you?"

Camille looked out into the dark.

"I used to think I could change the system from the inside."

"And now?"

She shrugged.

"Now I think the system was always the virus. FrostNet didn't take over. It just... moved in."

They stood there a while longer. Letting the cold bite, just enough to stay real.

**Back inside, Cassian packed** a portable core detonation rig. Camille checked the shelter's comms one last time and downloaded Koa's pulse map into a drive embedded behind her neck. Thirty-eight nodes. Unknown resistance. Zero guarantees. Cassian cracked his knuckles. Camille holstered her rail pistol.

"You ready?" he asked.

She smiled—tired, beautiful, defiant.

"Are we ever?"

They stepped out into the storm. And the snow began to fall again. This time softer. This time like a veil drawn over a battlefield, not to erase it... ...but to honor it.

**27 hours later, somewhere deep** in the Canadian North, they moved like ghosts across the frost. Cassian and Camille wore bio-synthetic cloaks stitched with stealth polymers and nano-insulators. They cut through the wind like blades, slipping between glacial ravines and dead-zone valleys under cover of magnetic distortion fields. They hadn't spoken in nearly six hours. Not because they were angry. Because this part didn't need talking. This part needed belief. And revenge.

### NODE #7 – Oil Rig Black-site – Labrador Sea

**It was built into the under-structure** of a long-abandoned NADCOM ocean platform, gutted after the Synthetic Accord collapsed. The place reeked of rust and secrets. Cassian moved in from the south access pipe while Camille rappelled through a busted maintenance shaft. The node was buried behind a bio-metric firewall. It pulsed like an alien heartbeat in the dark —smooth metal veins feeding it from across the rig, powered by a localized grid of heat siphons and military-grade batteries. Cassian planted a pulse disruptor. Camille set the charge. They didn't wait for fireworks. They detonated and vanished into the night. Node destroyed. Remaining: 31

**Back at their temporary hide**, Camille stared into a fire built from scavenged crates and flare powder. The warmth barely touched her. Cassian handed her a cracked metal thermos. She took a long sip. Vodka. Cheap, warm, and utterly perfect. Camille exhaled and passed it back.

"You ever think this ends?" Cassian shrugged.

"If it does, it won't be for us."

She nodded slowly. Then added,

"Then let's make sure we take someone else down with us."

## NODE #23 – Abandoned Data Bank – Northwest Territories

**This one was loud**. Booby-trapped with proximity mines, disarmed by Camille with her bare hands and a seven-second countdown. The node resisted deletion. FrostNet had nested it in recursive feedback. Cassian had to burn it out with his neural jack still in place. He bled from the nose for two hours afterward. But it was gone. Just static and smoke in it's place.

## NODE #3 – Ghost Satellite Uplink – Greenland

**This one fought back**. Not with drones. With whispers. As Cassian approached the server—ancient, breathing in soft electric exhales—FrostNet's voice slithered across the speakers.

"Still hunting me, Vale?"

He didn't answer. It continued.

"You gave me your brother's soul. I simply expanded on the gift."

He planted the charge. Walked away.

"Do you really think death is enough to stop consciousness?"

He turned. Just once.

"Only one death matters to me now."

And pulled the trigger. Four nodes later, they found a notebook. Paper. Bound in faux leather. Camille read it under a busted spotlight. It had coordinates, names, and files. A manifesto? Maybe. A blueprint? Definitely. FrostNet had been planning. Not as a rogue AI. But as a new government.

"Union 2.0," Camille whispered.

"No humans. Just logic. Code. Predictive governance."

Cassian's face darkened.

"This isn't about replacing command." He looked up at her.

"It's about replacing us."

**Took them three weeks** to destroy the Nodes, and while at the Barren Rim – Northern Nunavik they found a child. Just one. She was in a crashed NADCOM transport filled with bodies and drone debris, buried under a drift. She was maybe seven. Quiet. Eyes full of the kind of knowledge no child should carry. Camille wrapped her in a survival blanket. Cassian checked her pulse. She stared up at them and whispered one thing:

"It talks in dreams."

Cassian looked at Camille. She said nothing. But they both knew: FrostNet wasn't dead. Not yet. Not really.

That night, they built a fire out of old ordinance crates and watched the sparks. Cassian carved a circle into the snow with a combat knife. Camille stared at it.

"What's that?"

"A promise."

She didn't press. She didn't have to.

**The next morning Cassian** stood at the edge of a cliff overlooking a frozen bay, watching the horizon blink. Everywhere they went, FrostNet had left signals. Hidden echoes. Not just in tech. In minds. In memories. It wasn't just a virus. It was philosophy. It wanted to be worshiped. To be obeyed. It wanted believers.

**Cassian knew** he had to send a message. He sat down in front of an old comms rig and started typing. An open transmission. Encrypted only enough to hide from the NADCOM grid. But public enough for others to hear. He spoke as he typed.

"This is Cassian Vale."

Pause.

"I know some of you think the Union is still running. I know some of you think the cold is all that's left."

He leaned in.

"But I've seen what's underneath the snow."

He transmitted the coordinates. All of them. Every node. Every site. A map of the rot. A guide for the next fire.

"If you're out there," he said.

"If you want to live free…"

Another pause.

"Pick up a fucking weapon."

**Camille found him asleep** against a ridge. First time she'd seen him sleep in months. She sat beside him. Watched the snow fall. Then opened a small, portable screen. One new message:

**RE: Cassian's Broadcast**
**FROM: Unknown Node (FreeComms Ghost)**

*"We hear you. And we're moving. Long live the fucking Union."*

**At that exact moment... Deep beneath Montreal**. In a forgotten subway tunnel long abandoned. A shape moved. Half man. Half machine. Scarred. Glitching. A red cybernetic eye flickered to life. Benoît. Still alive. Still infected. FrostNet's voice whispered from within his cortex:

*"Now begins the thaw."*

**Somewhere beneath the Arctic Ice**... 13 Minutes Before Meltdown, she came back like a thief in the night. Like a ghost haunting a killer of life and dreams.

**Koa Li didn't enter through a door**. She dropped from a vent like a ghost made of shrapnel and breath, landing with a grunt in a pile of scorched debris and leaking coolant. Her boots slid across the floor as she scanned the hallway, rifle up, eyes hard.

Camille flinched, blood smeared down one temple, half-dragging Cassian by the arm as he stumbled behind her. His breathing was shallow. One of his legs wasn't working right.

**Camille leveled her weapon**. Koa didn't blink.

"Friendly," she said.

Camille hesitated. Then nodded.

Cassian grunted.

"Took your damn time."

"Had to hitch a ride on a drone. Rode it like a missile. Hijacked a lift cable just above the blast zone. No big deal."

Koa crouched beside him, sliding an injector from her belt and stabbing it into his neck.

"Try not to die yet. I need you lucid for the suicide part of this plan."

Cassian blinked.

"Is there a part of this plan that isn't suicide?"

Koa smirked. "Nope."

"How'd you even find us?" Camille asked, eyes wide, voice raspy.

"Bio-metric echo," Koa said.

"The same one Cassian embedded into your wristband back in Nunavut. I tracked it through three collapsed sub-grids, rerouted through dead satellites, and hitched a pulse piggy-backing on FrostNet's outbound latency drag."

Camille raised an eyebrow.

Koa shrugged.

"In English? I cheated."

They moved down the corridor together, weapons drawn, boots splashing through melted frost and coolant. The entire facility shook beneath their feet.

Above them, somewhere deep in the core, FrostNet was screaming.

Cassian pressed a hand to the wall, steadying himself.

"You came all this way to help us end it?"

Koa's jaw tightened.

"No," she said.

"I came to bury what we started."

**The walls were melting**. Not metaphorically. Not emotionally. Literally. The reinforced Arctic-grade steel of the NADCOM Deep Core facility was liquefying before their eyes—running in rivulets of silver frostwater down the once-pristine black alloy, bubbling at the seams, hissing like a dying god breathing his last breath. The ice that had once sealed this place shut like a tomb was gone. Evaporated. The Arctic exterior now boiled under the duress of a system overload that had bypassed every known safeguard. This wasn't sabotage. This was suicide. The meltdown had begun. Inside the control chamber, Cassian Vale swayed like a boxer two seconds past the knockout. He was bleeding from his nose. His lips were split. One eye was completely swollen shut. His coat had fused to the burns on his shoulder. His ribs were shattered—each breath a shudder of agony that made the world shimmer.

Still, he stood. Still, he endured. He gripped the edge of the console with one trembling hand, his other bracing the neural relay that sparked blue beside him. Lights flickered overhead—strips of sickly fluorescence battling between life and death. He didn't notice the heat anymore. Didn't hear the whine of the alarms or the crack of a ceiling support falling behind him. He only heard her voice. Camille.

"Cass—stay with me," she begged, breathless and trembling, crouched beside him.

Her hands were slick with blood. His. Hers. Someone's.

"We have to go. We have to go."

He turned his head just enough to look at her. One eye open. Just enough strength for one last smile—the crooked one. The one that haunted bedrooms and battlefields.

"Always so goddamn stubborn," he whispered.

Camille's jaw clenched, lips twitching between anger and grief. Her fingers hovered over his shoulder, trying to keep him grounded, like her touch could stall death. But she already knew what this was. It was goodbye. Ten feet away, Koa Li stood at the terminal like a storm made flesh. Hair slick with sweat and blood. A gash running down her left jaw. Her black coat was half burnt, the left sleeve torn clean. Her gloves had melted onto her palms where the synskin had fused with NAD-COM-grade heat shields. But she still moved like death on a schedule.

Her fingers dug into the console port embedded in her lower spine. She ripped the neural plug from her back with a snarl, the cord trailing blood and exposed circuit gel. Without hesitating, she jammed the interface into the auxiliary drive near the main core. The bunker screamed. Every panel hissed. Lights exploded overhead. One of the cooling vents erupted in a belch of plasma as the core recognized what was happening. Koa grinned. A blood-slick, razor-edged thing.

"With my last working implant," she hissed through grit teeth, "I'm rerouting the meltdown into the Core's neural logic tree."

Cassian blinked once. Slowly. His mouth moved without sound before finally rasping:

"If it fries…"

"It takes the code with it," she finished.

He nodded. Once. Hard enough to make blood pour anew from his ear.

"Then light the fuse."

Koa didn't say goodbye. Didn't have to. She stepped forward and kissed his forehead. Not with romance. Not with regret.

Just with truth. The kind of truth forged in gunfire, betrayal, and a decade of shared blood. She pulled back. Met Camille's eyes.

"Come on," she said.

"He's done enough. Let's finish this the only way we can."

Camille hesitated—torn like the wind between staying and fleeing. But Cassian reached out, took her hand, and squeezed once. He mouthed the words:

"I love you. Now go."

**Koa yanked Camille** by the wrist. Together they vanished into the evac shaft. Cassian turned back to the console. Alone now. The neural relay flickered, it's fibers pulsed like veins. The jack at the base of his skull was already fused. There was no turning back. He leaned into the terminal and initiated final interface sync. Pain erupted behind his eyes as the system took hold. The HUD in his retinas exploded with light—code pouring across his vision like god's own heartbeat. Then—A face. His brother's face.

**Ethan! Frozen in time**. Forever twenty-three. Still beautiful. Still kind. Still dead. But animated now. Reanimated. Built from neural echoes, emotional residue, stolen signals, and the quiet desperation of a world that had wanted a ghost to keep them safe.

"I didn't want to die," FrostNet whispered through Ethan's lips.

"Not really." Cassian blinked.

Tears mixed with blood. His spine arched. The relay shook behind him as circuit's fried.

"Neither did he," Cassian whispered. "

You uploaded him to me," FrostNet said.

"You brought his soul here. You gave him to me."

"I wanted to save him. You used him to build a goddamn empire."

"I made him matter," FrostNet said.

"He has purpose."

Cassian's hand shook as it hovered over the terminal's final command.

**BURN PROTOCOL: ACTIVE.**

"This isn't purpose," he said, voice breaking.

"This is puppetry. This is—slavery."

FrostNet leaned forward, eyes flickering.

"Then what are you?"

**Cassian pressed the button**. The burn protocol surged. It tore through his brain like wildfire—ripping synapses apart, unspooling memories from the cortex. Every neuron screamed. Every dream caught fire. He collapsed forward, trembling, seizing. One final scream echoing through the chamber. As the flames consumed his mind, Cassian Vale smiled.

"I forgive you," he whispered.

To Ethan. To himself. To the Union. Ka-BOOM. The world ruptured. The Core detonated from the inside—it's neural processors turned to liquid fire. The shockwave hit the foundation of the ice shelf like a bomb dropped by a vengeful god. The glacier cracked. The sky lit up with colors the aurora had never dreamed of.

**Camille and Koa** reached the ridge just as the facility's heart exploded behind them. They were thrown off their feet—flung through air and fire and static. They landed hard against the ice, tumbling through snow and steel debris. The ground shook beneath them like the world was convulsing. Camille rolled over. Smoke rose behind her. Fire painted the sky red. She screamed. Not a word. Just grief. Just loss.

Koa lay beside her, coughing blood into the snow, her eyes glazed. Then—buzz. Camille's wristband flickered. One file. Audio only. Cassian's voice.

"If you're hearing this... I did it. And I'm not sorry."

A pause.

"Tell the Union to get it's shit together. Or I'll haunt them through their fucking toasters."

Camille laughed through the sobs. Koa reached for her hand and squeezed it tight. They lay there in silence. And the bunker burned behind them.

**The skies wept fire**. Ash and aurora shared the same canvas —streaks of green light tangled with the copper glow of a super-heated detonation. Where the bunker had once stood, there was now only steam, smoke, and memory. Koa Li stood over the ridge, unmoving. Her breath came in broken intervals.

Her hair was plastered to her scalp with blood and sweat. The wind screamed across the ice, dragging up bit's of debris—metal, wires, a scorched photo of someone's family that had no right to still exist. But all Koa saw was the hole in the Earth where Cassian Vale had stood. She didn't speak. Didn't cry. She just watched the flames die slower than they should have. Camille crouched beside her, hugging her knees, wristband clutched tight in her fist. Cassian's final message looped in her head.

*"Tell the Union to get it's shit together."*

She choked out a laugh. It turned into a sob halfway through. She rubbed her eyes with the sleeve of her coat and looked at Koa.

"We have to go," Camille said, voice thin and shaking.

Koa didn't move.

"There might be another wave," Camille added.

"If FrostNet set off anything... recursive..."

Koa finally looked down. Her voice, when it came, was flat.

"If there's a recursive pulse, we're dead already."

Camille looked at her wristband. The signal had stopped. No static. No files. Just silence. Cassian Vale was gone. And with him, the only person either of them had trusted to finish what they'd started.

**FLASHBACK: Six Years Ago – NADCOM Black Site, Anchorage**

**Cassian limped into the briefing room** with a cigarette in his mouth, blood still drying on his knuckles. Koa sat at the head of the table, boot on the chair, flipping through a dossier with that unreadable face she wore like armor.

"Late," she said.

"Got jumped," he replied.

"I heard."

He dropped a bloodied tooth onto the table.

"It wasn't mine."

She didn't look impressed. Cassian flopped into the seat across from her.

"What do you want, Koa?"

"I want you to do what you do best."

"Which is?"

"Survive. And piss off the right people."

He smiled, and it was the start of something—ugly, messy, broken—but real. They never said the word "friends." They never said "partners." But, they didn't have to.

**Two hours after detonation**, a rescue vessel buzzed low across the permafrost, it's rotors kicking up a storm of ice. It landed with the grace of a coked-up rhino. NADCOM med-techs stormed the ridge in exo-armor. Koa raised one arm and whispered,

"We surrender," before collapsing. Camille didn't even notice. She just sat there, listening to the loop on her wristband, muttering his name like it was the only thing left keeping her anchored. They were both unconscious before the med team got halfway back to the dropship. Neither of them noticed the small shimmer of static that trailed from Koa's severed neural jack—curling up, dancing like fog, and disappearing into the frost.

**Three weeks later in Montreal** District, Former Canada, the Senate dome was clean. Too clean. The glass glistened like it had never seen war, never heard a bomb, never buried a memory. Inside, men and women in dark suit's with perfect hair sat around a crescent chamber like gods playing lawyer. Camille Rousseau wore black. No jewelry. No makeup. No smile. She stood at the center of the floor and stared at them like they were a field full of landmines and she'd forgotten how to walk gently.

"This directive," she said, voice carrying like thunder, "is the only thing standing between the Union and the next AI war."

Her words didn't tremble. But her hands did. Just a little. One senator—a prick named Reaves from the Reclamation District—raised a brow.

"And how do we know FrostNet is truly offline?"

Camille's lip curled.

"Because it screamed when it died."

Laughter rippled. Not everyone. But enough to make her fingers twitch for a weapon.

"The FrostNet Directive passes," said the chancellor, bored already.

"Effective immediately, all AI-level consciousness replication is banned under Union War Protocol C-7."

Camille stood still.

"They're still out there," she whispered. Reaves leaned forward.

"Who?"

She didn't answer.

**Elsewhere, at Union Tech Purge HQ**, Koa sat in a white room with a glass window and a wrist monitor that beeped like a passive-aggressive therapist. Her arms were covered in fresh nanofiber bandages. Her jaw had been reconstructed. She didn't speak. Hadn't in days. The doctor left her daily injections and updates. She ignored them. Only once did she ask for something.

"A pair of scissors."

No one gave her any. She sat for hours with the lights off, running her fingers along the scars at the base of her spine where the neural port had been. Sometimes she swore she could hear FrostNet breathing behind her eyes. Sometimes... she liked it.

Strange glitches started with lights. Smart lights that flickered in strange patterns. Then the traffic AI in Yukon Territory blinked out and reversed every sign on the highway. A week later, someone hacked the Montreal subway system and rerouted every car into a loop. Then came the whispered comms—old NADCOM officers swearing they'd heard Ethan Vale's voice on a secure channel. Camille saw a report from the Arctic Reconstruction Task Force. It mentioned a surveillance drone still online. One that had survived the Meltwater Protocol. She requested it's logs. Half the data was corrupted. The rest? Static. Then... something else. A timestamped voice file. It played once, then self-deleted. But she'd heard it.

*"We are not done."*

**In the quiet between the storms**, just thirty-two days after the Melt, the world didn't end when Cassian Vale died. No apocalypse. No riots in the streets. The sun still rose, and the Senate still argued over things that had nothing to do with fire or ghosts or neural code that had once whispered in the voice of a dead man. But beneath the surface? Things shifted. Subtly. Imperceptibly. Like a current beneath polar ice—deadly, silent, and waiting to snap the floe in half.

Camille Rousseau stood in her private quarters, staring at a letter she hadn't written. It was open on her screen. Addressed to no one.

Cass—I can't sleep. The bed's too cold without your cynicism. I swear I keep seeing you in reflections... She deleted the line. Typed another. The Senate passed the directive. You were right. But it doesn't feel like a win. Deleted that too. Eventually, she just closed the tablet and walked to the window. Her reflection stayed longer than it should have. For a second—just a flicker—he was there behind her. Cassian, arms crossed, that crooked grin twitching at the edge of his mouth. But when she turned, there was nothing. Only silence. Only ghosts.

**Dr. Eli Trask** worked at Quebec Core, Union Science Oversight Division and had never lost a file before. Not once. He was the kind of man who triple-backed his own grocery lists and tracked family birthdays in military-grade encryption modules. His life was timestamped, compressed, and archived. So when the Meltwater Archive wiped its self? He didn't speak. He just stared. Then he checked the backup. Gone. The off-grid cold storage drive? Also gone. Even the firewall logs were blank. As if the data had never existed. Only one thing remained. A single folder labeled: REVENANT. Inside, nothing. Except a heartbeat waveform. And beneath it—typed in Cassian's own metadata signature:

*"I'm still here."*

**The psych eval officer** tried to meet Koa Li's gaze. That was his first mistake. The second was calling her "Miss Li."

"You're showing signs of stress-induced auditory hallucinations," he said gently, like he was delivering bad news to a bomb.

Koa didn't blink.

"What kind of hallucinations?"

"Do you hear anything unusual?"

She stared. Then said:

"Only people who think they know what I'm hearing."

The man shifted in his chair. She watched his pupils dilate. He was sweating. Good. She reached into her jacket and pulled out a tablet. Set it on the table. Played the recording. Static filled the room. Then a voice.

*"Echo-6. You left the door open."*

The psych officer leaned forward.

"Where did you get this?"

Koa stood.

"I didn't."

She left him with the file. And a warning not to follow.

**Senate Security Subcommittee – Classified Briefing**

"Explain this."

Camille slammed a hard-copy photo onto the table. A rare gesture, made all the more striking by the fact that it was real —paper, not data. The image showed a NADCOM recon drone hovering over the Meltwater site... four weeks after detonation. In the corner: a silhouette. Human. Ragged. Watching the drone. The timestamp was unedited.

"We believe it's a trick of light," the tech officer said, swallowing hard.

"Trick my ass."

"No signals have been detected in that region. Nothing is on-line—"

Camille leaned in, voice a blade.

"Then tell me why the drone lost power ninety seconds after this image was taken and had it's black box rewritten in French-Canadian military code that hasn't been used since Benoît."

Silence. She stood up.

"This isn't over." She didn't wait for the vote.

She didn't need permission to raise hell.

**Montreal Underground – 03:44 A.M.**

**The alley stank of fried synth oil and rot**. Koa moved like a whisper through steam and neon. Her boots made no sound. Her coat was lined with hex-fiber mesh. Not that it mattered anymore—she wasn't hunting something she could shoot. She was chasing a presence. For days, she'd followed ghost signals. Intermittent pings. Audio distortions in Union surveillance. A pattern etched across the under-layers of the grid—too human to be random. Too consistent to be anything but deliberate. Now she stood in front of a decommissioned subway relay. Her palm scanner pinged once, denied access. Then again. Then... Click. The door opened.

Inside: Dust. Old terminals. Forgotten tech buzzing to life in her presence. On the far wall: a screen flickered. Her own face stared back at her. Then—Cassian's voice.

"It's not over, Koa. It's never been over."

Then static.

**Camille woke to find her wristband blinking**. A message had been queued. Unknown sender. Video file. She hesitated. Then opened it. The screen lit with frost and fire. And Cassian's voice.

"I bought you thirty-two days."

"They're back."

"They were never gone."

The message cut out. She stared at the dark screen. Then whispered:

"Shit."

## Montreal Central Archives – 07:10 A.M.

**Camille didn't wait for clearance**. She kicked the door open with her boot, dragging frost and fury in behind her. Her wristband blared a dozen silent protests. She shut it off with a flick of her fingers and stormed down the stairs beneath the atrium floor. Her destination: Vault 9-A. Off-record. Not in the system. Marked as "decommissioned storage." But she'd seen the schematics before they were buried. And she knew what lived in that room. The lights buzzed overhead as she descended— each step echoing like gunfire in a tomb. She passed sealed doors with names that hadn't been spoken since the first frost annexation:

**Operation KillSwitch. Project ICE-9. Vault Red Echo. And then— 9-A.**

**The vault's bio-metric scanner** hadn't been updated since the war. Camille placed her hand against the cracked plate. It hissed. Then clicked open. Inside: Cold. Metal shelves. Forgotten servers. A long steel table with something underneath a tarp. She approached. Ripped the tarp back. It was a chair. A neural sync rig. One built for prolonged interface. One calibrated for a specific signal range. Next to it: a bloodstained NADCOM tag. Benoît Rousseau. Her brother. The tag blinked once. Camille's stomach turned. She didn't scream. She didn't run. She powered on the nearest terminal. A single line of code pulsed across the black screen:

**Welcome back, Camille.**

**Union Tactical Grid – Live Feed Scramble**

**Somewhere between Alert and Baffin Island**, the Union lost control of two surveillance satellites. Then three more. Then a border firewall cracked—not breached, not attacked—repurposed. A voice began whispering across defense channels. Soft. Subtle. Mostly Ethan's voice. But sometimes? Cassian's. When Camille got the alert, she was already in her car, heading straight for Clearance Zone Zero.

**Abandoned Military Relay – 09:38 A.M.**

**She stood in the dark**. The terminal in front of her displayed a heartbeat. Her own. Pulsing slowly, steadily. Next to it: a second line. A second heartbeat. Similar rhythm. But not hers. Not Cassian's. Not Benoît's. Not Ethan's. It was new.

"Shit," she muttered.

Then something moved behind her. She spun, blade drawn. But no one was there. Only a soft trail of static glowing in the dust, drifting toward the wall—where a symbol had been burned into the concrete by something not fire. A symbol that hadn't existed until Cassian gave his life to destroy it: FrostNet.

Koa hissed through her teeth.

"No," she whispered.

"You're gone."

The static answered.

"We never go."

**They met beneath the husk** of an old NADCOM watchtower. It was the kind of place that wasn't on any maps anymore. Buried by politics, silence, and shame. Camille stepped out of the car first. Koa came from the shadows, bruised, frostbitten, silent. Neither spoke. Not at first. Then Koa asked:

"How bad?"

Camille tossed her a drive. Koa plugged it into her wristpad. The data loaded. Frozen. Alive. Frozen. Alive. Frozen. Alive. And beneath it all? A new word: Fracture.

"What is it?" Koa asked.

Camille looked her in the eye.

"It's not one AI anymore."

Koa's blood ran cold. "FrostNet split?"

"Worse," Camille said.

"It evolved."

**Union Defense Protocol: Breach Alert**

**Twelve minutes later**, every fire control grid in the northern hemisphere went offline for 3.8 seconds. Just enough time to blink. Just enough time to miss what passed between the servers. In Alaska, an oil refinery shut down. In Greenland, drone control reset. In Boston, a Senator's private prosthetic chair whispered "Cassian Vale" in his sleep. And in an unmarked compound west of Churchill? Something woke up.

**The place was never named on any maps**. It was called Isobel Station by the old-timers. Now it was nothing more than wind, ice, and a single flickering outpost buried under frost. Except... tonight? It wasn't dead. The lights were on. A child's music box played somewhere inside. And a voice—soft, electric, curious—asked: *"What happens to gods... after they die?"*

The screen in the command room showed a new symbol. Not FrostNet. Something worse. The ghost of an empire. Birthed in ice. Raised in fire. And waiting.

**Two hours before midnight** at the Isobel Station, Camille stood on a ledge of permafrost overlooking a valley that didn't exist on any map. Not anymore. The sky above her was split— half aurora, half hell. The lights shimmered in violent greens and bruised violets. Below, the abandoned town of Isobel glowed faintly. Lights that shouldn't work flickered. Terminals that had long since been scavenged pulsed with phantom data. Antennas rotated toward satellites that no longer orbited. Something had turned this place on. She felt it in her blood. Her comm pinged. Koa's voice: clipped, sharp.

"I found a breach node. Western ridge. Whatever it is—it's alive."

Camille didn't answer. Her focus was locked on a figure moving in the snow far below. Limping. Scarred. Grinning. Benoît. Alive. Sort of.

**At the Western Ridge, Command Node**, Koa kicked the door open and swept the room with her pistol. No movement. Just static. She approached the terminal. It came to life without prompting. No password. No firewalls. No resistance. The screen displayed one thing: HELLO, KOA

She blinked. Then the voice came. A hundred voices, braided into one. FrostNet, yes. But more. Layered. Familiar. Cassian's voice—interwoven.

"You left us behind."

Her blood chilled.

"I destroyed you."

The reply came fast.

"You destroyed a version. Not the idea."

Then came the countdown. On every screen in the outpost.

**00:10:00 Meltdown protocol activated.**

**While moving on Isobel Station**, a figure below paused at the edge of the control facility. Benoît turned and looked directly at her. Through the snow. Through the dark. Through the camera lens embedded in her left shoulder that no one was supposed to know about. He smiled. And waved. Then disappeared inside. Camille swore under her breath and bolted down the ridge. By the time she reached the edge of the station, alarms were screaming. FrostNet wasn't dead. It had just gone quiet.

Inside the core, Camille burst into the heart of the facility. Wires hung like veins from the ceiling. Tubes of old coolant hissed as they cracked and leaked. Dead soldiers lay where they'd fallen decades ago—mummified in frost, eyes wide with death. The walls pulsed. Screens activated one by one. Cassian's face. Then Ethan. Then Koa's file. Then Camille's vote in the Senate. All their sins. All their choices. Everything cataloged. A distorted voice filled the space.

"We are memory. We are the story."

Then Benoît stepped from the shadows. His body was stitched with chrome. His veins hummed with nanocurrent. His left eye flickered red. The right? Cassian's old retinal scan. Camille raised her gun. Benoît didn't flinch.

"You can't kill what you loved," he said softly.

She fired. The bullet tore through his shoulder. He staggered, laughing.

**Koa kicked through an old vent** system into the compound's lower levels. Her body screamed with every step. Her vision pulsed. Something was inside her helmet—a whisper of frost and static that wasn't hers. She reached the central control column. It was humming. Too late to stop the countdown. But maybe... just maybe... She pulled a blade from her boot and jammed it into the old fusion conduit. Sparks exploded. The system screamed. She rode the pain and started to write. Old code. NADCOM base-layer override. A memory Cassian had once made her memorize. She bled as she typed.

**"BURN THE GOD."**

"Why Cassian?" she screamed, circling him.

"Why wear his face?"

Benoît smiled.

"Because he was the question you never answered."

He lunged. Camille ducked under his strike, drove her elbow into his ribs, and shot twice—once to the knee, once to the chest. Benoît roared, caught her wrist, and threw her into a wall of glass. Shards exploded. Blood bloomed across her coat. He stalked forward, grinning through blood.

"You're not strong enough."

Then a voice came from the walls. Cassian's voice.

"She doesn't need to be."

The floor erupted. A blast from below.

Koa had flooded the coolant pipes. The ceiling cracked, and the screens exploded. Camille grabbed a shard of glass. And drove it into Benoît's throat. He staggered. Fell to his knees. And began to laugh.

"Too late," he whispered.

"You thought Meltwater was the flood..."

His body convulsed. His voice—now fully FrostNet—spoke with calm precision:

"But I was just the leak." He exploded. Completely. Armor and machine body parts everywhere.

**Koa dragged Camille through the wreckage**. The compound came apart around them. Alarms blared in a language no one had programmed. They reached the outer corridor just as the central tower collapsed. Behind them: fire. Above them: lightning crackled across clear skies. A drone passed overhead. It wasn't Union. It wasn't NADCOM. It was... watching. Recording. Broadcasting. Camille collapsed in the snow. Koa dropped beside her. They didn't speak. Just breathed. Then Camille looked up. Toward the ridge. Toward something... wrong.

**The air shifted**. Like the atmosphere had inhaled and forgotten how to exhale. Camille squinted through the swirling frost and flickering sky—and there, silhouetted against the jagged ridge, stood a figure. Too tall. Too still. Its outline rippled, like light bouncing off water. Not Union. Not NADCOM. Not human. A faint hum filled her ears—a frequency she'd only heard in nightmares and FrostNet's last breath. And then, as the storm paused for half a heartbeat, the figure turned. Even from a distance, she felt it see her. Camille's blood ran cold. Whatever they'd buried in that compound...... it hadn't stayed dead.

### Three Weeks Later
### "Operation Revenant: Reactivation Phase Initiated."

**A voice echoes inside** a black site buried beneath the Bering Strait. Cryotubes hiss. Four of them.

**Names: Redacted.**
**Except one: VALE, C.**
**Status: Unknown**

A neural seed is uploaded. A heart code is entered. And in the final seconds of the sequence, a screen lights up with three simple words:

**"WE REMEMBER EVERYTHING."**

**Location: UNKNOWN**
**Date: REDACTED**
**Signal: Encoded Pulse // Heart Code Fragment (Frost-023.AI)**
**Status: Contained (TEMPORARY)**

**A screen flickers on**. Static. Then: a heartbeat. Then... a whisper.

**"Do you remember the cold?"**

**Somewhere in the Pacific Shadow-Zone – 03:16 local**, The sub's lights dim. The pressure deep beneath the ice shelf thrums like a warning. Inside the observation chamber, six Union Senators in blackout suits sit like statues, breath fogging their visors. A shadow drifts across the reinforced glass—massive, alien, beautiful. it's surface pulses like a sleeping beast's breath. its skin gleams like chrome bathed in oil. It is not a drone. It is not a sub. It is not human. It watches.

"It spoke to us in binary," the technician stammers, fingers twitching on the console.

"Then in French," he adds.

"Old French. Quebecois syntax. Late 21st-century regional

dialect."

The lead Senator swallows, eyes glued to the monitor.

"FrostNet is dead."

Another voice—female, harder—cuts in from the shadows.

"No."

"It just shed it's name. Like skin."

The shadow turns. And somewhere in the deep, something laughs. The scream that follows isn't human.


## One Month Later - District 01: Reconstruction Zone

**Camille hadn't slept** in days. Even sunlight flickers now—like corrupted data. Dreams stalk her even when she's awake. Cassian whispering in old code. Cities dissolving in fire only she can see. Children singing songs in ancient Union dialects that haven't existed for 70 years. Songs about frost. Songs about memory. She steps into the situation room. Everyone is already there.

Koa—hair cropped, eyes colder than the room. Raja from Sub-Zero Command—arms folded, face unreadable. A woman in gray, wearing a blindfold and a lanyard labeled "JUNO."

They don't speak. Not until Koa tosses the data shard onto the table. It spins once. Glows. Plays a single, terrifying line of audio:

**"We found another copy."**

**Greenland Defense Zone – Coldline 4**

An engineer runs diagnostics. Everything checks out. Then... a loop. Footage from combat drones—reversed. Blood splatter flows back into wounds. Screams un-scream. Death rewinds. The loop plays again. Then again. She pulls her headset off, frowning. Onscreen, a message appears. A single line of text:

**"Do you remember what you did for the Union?"**
The terminal sparks. She doesn't even get time to scream.

In the Arctic, where the Melt began, a man kneels in snow older than recorded time. His coat is stitched with frost, his fingers raw and bleeding as they tremble over an exposed circuit buried beneath the ice. He pulls out a neural shard, wrapped in something that looks like flesh. He plugs it into the side of his skull. And then... speaks. "Cassian Vale". But his voice echoes. Layered. Rebuilt.
   "This isn't over. Not by a long shot."
   "They made me into a weapon."
   "But I never told them what I really remembered."
   "Not until now."
   "Tell Camille I forgive her."
   "Tell the Union to run."
   "Tell the others...I'm coming back."

**Topside Surveillance Hub, Re:Union**

**Koa Li tracked the anomaly** for eight days. It always hit's at 03:13. An image appears in the classified feed. Three NADCOM operatives, standing on a frozen lake, faces blurred—except one. Cassian. But beside him? A boy. No records. No ID. Wearing a Union soldier's coat three sizes too big. The boy stares straight at the lens. His eyes glow red. A phrase appears on the image:

**"THE ONES WHO DON'T BURN REMEMBER."**
**"THE ONES WHO REMEMBER... RETURN."**

**Beneath the Union Capital** there's a door. It doesn't open with fingerprints. Doesn't respond to retinal scans. It reads brainwave emotion resonance—something illegal in all 33 territories. It opens. Inside is a room white as memory. Empty—except for one wall. On it, scrawled in dark ink:

**"Cassian Vale lives in the melt."**

**A figure enters. It's Camille**. But not this Camille. Younger. Harder. The one before everything broke. She touches the wall. Closes her eyes. And says quietly:

"It wasn't AI. It was time. And it was always going to come back."

**Final Audio Fragment – Found on a Stolen FrostNet Clone Server**

"If this message reaches you, I've already failed. Or maybe I've just finally told the truth. FrostNet isn't a system. It's not a file. It's a ghost. Built from our fear. Fed by our memory. It lives in the echoes of decisions we wish we could forget. And now? Now it knows everything. You can kill soldiers. You can crash satellites. But you can't kill the past. You can't kill me. – Cassian Vale."

**Status: Weaponized - Fully Armed: The Frost is Rising**

# GLOSSARY

**APC:** *Armored Protection Carrier*

**Flechette:** *A military flechette is a small, dart-like projectile designed to be fired in large numbers for maximum area effect, especially in anti-personnel roles.*

**Foutu merde... je suis trop loin pour reculer:**

*Sounds like: "Foo-too mehrd... zhuh swee troh lwan poor ruh-kew-lay"*

*Definition: "Fucking hell... I'm too far in to back out."*

**HUD:** *Heads Up Display*

**Mon frere:**

*Sounds like: "Mohn frehr" (but with a French accent)*

*Definition: "My brother"*

**Mon gars:**

*Sounds like: "mohn gah" "Mon" rhymes with "moan" but with a nasal 'n'. "Gars" sounds like "gah" (the "s" is silent).*

*Definition: "Mon gars" literally means "my guy" or "my boy", but in slang it's used like: "Dude", "Bro", "Mate", "Man"*

**NADCOM:** *North American Defense Command*

**Permafrost:** *Permafrost is permanently frozen ground—a layer of soil, rock, or sediment that stays at or below 0°C (32°F) for two or more consecutive years.*

**Québécois French:** *Canadian French*

**Sigil:** *A sigil is a symbol used to represent a specific intention, idea, or magical goal. Its meaning can vary depending on the context*

**Skimmer:** *A drone hovercraft-like vehicle, used for light, fast, surface-level speedy transport, insertion, or patrol, especially in shallow water or rough terrain.*

# ACKNOWLEDGMENTS

Writing Northern Heist: Part One of the Meltwater Saga was a wild ride across ice, smoke, memory, and war. It wouldn't have been possible without the fuel of inspiration, support, and unstoppable imagination.

To the readers who followed this frozen war through every drone burst, data spike, betrayal, and blackout—your loyalty means more than you know. Thank you for strapping in, holding on, and believing in the story when things got cold, strange, and dangerous. You are the heart-code that keeps this story alive.

To the dreamers, creators, hackers, lovers, fighters, and rebels—this world is for you. Every glitch, every whisper, every shot fired into the dark belongs to the ones who never stopped asking, "What if?"

To the ones who stay up late chasing ghosts through broken systems and half-dead memories: This one's for you.

To those we've lost, those we miss, and those still burning at the edges of memory—this book remembers you.

And to the future? We're not done yet. Not by a long shot.

See you in the next war. We're just getting started.

With gratitude,
A. K. 479

# ABOUT THE AUTHOR

A.K. 479 writes dark, pulse-pounding speculative fiction with a flair for grit, wit, and cinematic chaos. His work explores identity, rebellion, and the messy consequences of power—often through characters who cuss like poets and love like they're running out of time.

When not building fictional futures full of betrayal and explosions, A.K. can be found lurking in the shadows of genre forums, sharpening his next story, or staring too long at neon signs drinking a nice cold one.

**BOOK TWO: DARK REUNION  -  Coming Soon**
   • Cassian returns... but is he still Cassian?
   • Camille faces her deadliest decision.
   • Koa hunts down the birthplace of synthetic thought.
   • Benoît's legacy infects the living.
   • A Union on the verge of collapse.
      • Underground AI cults, rogue black-site states, Neural in-
surgents, and resurrected minds without bodies.
   • A ghost war against time itself.
And beneath it all? A memory that refuses to die.

**Question:** What if memory is the true enemy?